# JOSEPHINE

{ *'an open book'* }

## ANGELA DOUGLAS

CANDY JAR BOOKS · CARDIFF
2018

Printed and bound in the UK
by 4edge, 22 Eldon Way, Hockley, Essex, SS5 4AD

ISBN: 978-1-9125350-8-8

Published by
Candy Jar Books
Mackintosh House
136 Newport Road, Cardiff, CF24 1DJ
www.candyjarbooks.co.uk

*For Bill, my sweet love,*
*and*
*in memory of Daddy, Mummy and Kenny*

*The past is a memory.*
*It must be looked at in the light of former days.*
Irish proverb

*Mosaics, small fragments of memories scatter, I'm reaching for them, but I'm not sure: are they your dreams... mine? All the moments that might have been, all of the if only moments. Like stepping stones across a river.*

# Prologue

When do moments become memories? I was eight years old. Eight years old… When the days seemed endless. With my brother, Johnnie, I'd run through the park, Lady, our small black poodle, yapping at our heels. When we heard Mummy calling us, we would hide, then, when we thought it was safe, skip down to the crumbling ruin of the house on the corner. Bombed to a shell during the war, it was slowly being reclaimed by nature, saplings and briars, ferns and shoots twisting and clinging their way upwards through plaster and stone. Daddy told me that, long before I was born, it had been the home of the Duke of Windsor and his Duchess. Now it was home only to feral cats, which hissed at us as we stumbled and scrambled our way, searching for chick weed to treat Dickie, our budgie.

When you were eight years old… Ah, a bee fixes on an English rose. I'm thinking of my friend Liz. I can see her now, her head of thick, blonde hair. Her face tilted towards mine. Her voice…

'Josephine, if you can let go of your past, your past will let go of you.'

I tell her that the past is the present and the future too.

# One

Home was a five-storey period house in a smart west London street. My parents had bought a short lease on a ground and lower-ground floor flat – three bedrooms, a kitchen, a bathroom and a living room. Cramped for the five of us, with no back garden for Lady, but as my father liked to remind us, 'a good address'. We were working class with middle class aspirations. Money was often too tight to mention, and sometimes Daddy's shouting made Mummy cry, turning little girls' hearts into jellies in their sides. But it was the '50s. A moment ago the world had been at war – times were tough for all but a few.

My bedroom was at the end of a short corridor on the first floor. It would have been a good size if it had been all mine, but it had been divided into two halves: one for me and my single bed, the other with a bunk for Johnnie. There was space enough in my half for my clothes to hang, a wooden prayer chair, and sitting on a long shelf under my window, my teddy bear, my collection of small china squirrels, my books and my records, and a tin music box with Prince Charming and Cinderella holding each other close. With a twist of the key they would twirl around to the tune of 'The Loveliest Night of the Year' – or so my mother told me; the key had been long lost.

When I snuggled down to sleep, my arms tucked under the blankets for warmth, the last thing I would see was a black and white photograph of Elvis Presley, pinned up directly in my eye line, signed 'To Sweet Josephine, I love you too', followed by three kisses. Love to me from me.

On the far side of the room there was a tall window. If I leaned out as far as I could, I could see down into the kitchen. See our sweet old family life in a capsule, as though a stage had been set for a play.

I can see Andrew, my handsome Irish daddy, reed thin and tall, with the brightest of blue eyes, thick hair and the most beautiful hands ever seen on a man. Standing by the old stone butler's sink, he peers into the small round mirror on the wall as he shaves. He straightens, his braces hanging down over his high-waisted trousers, and sings a snatch of song from the twenties.

I can see my English mummy, slight and reserved, a beauty still, with her green eyes and long dark hair, leaning over her sewing machine. Groping around for her cigarettes, she scolds Johnnie for teasing Lady.

And nineteen-year-old Ellen, in all her gorgeousness, combing her dark curls. Full shiny skirt with swishing petticoat, tiny waist and bosoms bouncing, she waits by the door for her latest crush to call.

I press my nose against the window. My breath fogs the glass. They loved me, as I loved them.

As the Irish say: I have Josephine from my godmother and Nancy from my Granny in Galway. So here I am, Josephine Cagney, and I'm leaving this all behind.


Daddy always believed I'd have a sparkling future. Wasn't I pretty, couldn't I sing, didn't I love to dance? 'She's a dead cert,' he'd say to anyone who would listen. 'Look, she has Betty Grable's legs! She's the sort of girl who'd wear a red dress to a funeral!'

Mummy had other ideas. 'No theatre for you, young lady. You're sixteen now, time for a proper job.'

While waiting in the doctor's surgery, she'd seen an advertisement in *The Lady*. A family in Kensington Square needed a young girl to assist the nanny in the care of twin four-year-old girls. Knowing my love of children, she'd spoken to the head housekeeper on my behalf. An appointment had been made for me to be interviewed.

Daddy was more than miffed at the idea – 'She'll have enough of wiping her own babies' bottoms without having to wipe other people's!' – but Mummy was implacable, and in the end he simply shrugged his shoulders. Anything for a quiet life.

So it was that on the first Sunday of May, Mummy and I made our way by bus to the other side of Hyde Park. My hair in a page boy cut, fringe pinned back clear of my forehead, I was wearing black shoes with Louis heels, stockings with seams and my new grey flannel suit made for me by my mother for just such a special occasion.

Number fifteen was a grand grey building covered with wisteria. Nervously we climbed the black and white tiled steps leading to the imposing front door. Tentatively we tapped the knocker, a polished-brass lion's head,

3

twice.

The door was opened by a woman of about fifty-five, who introduced herself as Mrs Robertson, the house keeper. Her face was a pale round tea plate, with eyes like two bright brown buttons. I sensed her glancing me over as she asked us into a small room off the main hall.

Closing the door firmly behind her, she made sure we were sitting comfortably, close enough to each other for Mummy to hold my hand.

'So, you are Josephine?' she asked kindly.

I nodded meekly.

'What have you been doing since you left school?'

'I've been taking dancing and singing classes.'

Mrs Robertson's eyebrows arched. 'So why do you now want to become a nanny?'

I hesitated. 'Well… I love children and… my parents want me to have a proper job.'

I looked to Mummy for support. She squeezed my hand. My pulse thumping under her fingers, she leaned forward in her chair. 'Josephine's a good girl, Mrs Robertson,' she said, 'Never had a moment's trouble with her.' She smoothed down her skirt and sighed. 'She's nervous today, seems to have lost her tongue.' Her voice was mild and full of affection. 'We just want the best for her. For her to be secure.'

I would never have believed that one family could need so many people just to keep their lives ticking over. The Nerstmore family employed a chauffeur, a nanny, a housekeeper, a cook and, skipping into my new life, me. And that was just those of us who lived in. Then there was the valet, the secretary who came in for two mornings a week, two daily cleaners and a part time gardener. You'd have thought the house would be a hive of activity, but apart from the nursery and the kitchen, it was hushed. I seldom met my fellow staff, and if I did they seemed like novice nuns padding about in a convent.

Nanny Ford and I didn't hit it off straight away. Small with a tired, knotted face, she'd stand in the doorway watching me every minute of the day. I was a clean slate and I was to be her project. 'I've told you, not that way.' 'Only half a job done there, Josephine child!' 'Oh, you haven't starched their knickers as well?' Shrugging her shoulders in irritation: 'No salt on their carrots!' 'Have you checked the time table, the lists?'

She'd rattle those lists off in her shrill voice till I thought I'd go bonkers. You couldn't say I wasn't trying. By the end of the day I'd feel like a wet rag.

4

I hardly ever saw Lady Salina, and when I was finally introduced, I found her to be almost without expression. Bright and polished, tall and thin, she was all jutting hip bones and stringy arms. I thought she must have lived on grapefruit and hard boiled eggs. Her immaculate strawberry blonde hair, clipped behind one ear, swung artfully to one side as she raised her chin to look down her nose at you. I'd seen pictures in magazines of women like her. I'd questioned my mother: why were they always talked about as if we were supposed to know who they were? Mrs Rogers, Lady Whatsit, Dame Something-or-other...

'But who *are* they?' I'd ask.

'It's what's done,' I was assured.

Lady Salina looked me over with dispassionate eyes. Did I intend to stay in my post long? The last one hadn't lasted long, no more than two months. Very tiresome. Children don't like changes to their routine.

Neither did her Ladyship, it would seem.

I was to follow Nanny's rules. If I had any problems I shouldn't bother her, but speak to Mrs Robertson. Her Ladyship needed her rest. I wondered if this was what a soft life did to a woman. She reached for a cigarette and, with a flick of her gold Cartier lighter, bade me a brief good morning. You wouldn't have seen my heels for dust.

The twins, Alice and Grace, were the sunniest of miracles. Pale copper curls with milky skin and dimpled little arms – you just wanted to take a bite. They were into everything they ought not to have been. I was dizzy with keeping my eye on them. Alone in the nursery I'd teach them to sing – 'Rose Marie' or 'True Love' – and to dance along, and we'd lark around while they slobbered me with kisses. We dressed them in matching outfits: smocked Liberty print dresses with matching knickers and little white ankle socks and their red Mary Jane shoes. They'd look the perfect picture when Nanny took them down to the drawing room for their hour with their parents. I wondered why people bothered having babies if they only wanted to pass them over to others to soothe them to sleep.

The days of playing out in the garden with Alice and Grace were golden times. The garden was my sanctuary in the city. Apart from the little ones I could be alone there, though sometimes I would encounter his Lordship. I'd been told he was a military man. He'd had what was called a 'good war'. I've always believed that was the most insensitive thing one could say about the dead.

Tall, with a big belly and neat dark hair cut too short and combed back from his forehead, his Lordship always seemed to be deep in thought. I would first become aware of him when the girls took off, running to him, calling 'Papa, Papa!' with peals of laughter. It would have been heart-warming if he'd ever gathered them into his arms.

'Precious,' he'd say, smoothing their hair. It was comical to see him trying to walk away with dignity, a child wrapped around each leg. I'd busy myself putting dolls back in their prams, returning the trike to its place, thinking, *quick*, straighten your dress, tighten up your pony tail.

Sometimes he came over to speak to me. 'Well,' he might ask, 'you enjoy my garden?'

'Sir, I… I love flowers that smell,' I'd say, with a little rush of confidence.

Always short, empty snatches of polite pleasantness like this – no witticisms, though once he did ask me, turning and gesturing back at the house, 'Do you enjoy the fine views over London from your room?'

I explained that my window was too high up for me to see out from. I smiled carefully at him, and he smiled back. I waited. If he didn't say anything to me, was it my place to babble away? It appeared not. There was a short silence, like an indrawn breath. His Lordship's mind seemed suddenly elsewhere, and he turned away, clearing his throat, and walked back towards the house.

I wondered if men like him found peace as difficult as war.

On my afternoons off I'd wander along to Kensington High Street and browse the record shop. As I flicked through the records, I would chat to a friendly girl who worked there. Liz was a little older than me, taller, with bleach-blonde hair that Mummy would have called 'common'. She was from Essex, a dancer, and she had the singing voice of an angel. But if I secretly nursed dreams of my own name in lights, of the warmth of the spotlight, Liz was perfectly happy where she was. In her lunch hour we'd go to the new coffee bar nearby. We'd sit on high stools, swinging our legs like American girls in a movie, tuck into our Wimpy burgers and suck on the straws of our strawberry Whipsys. In those moments, I felt my new life was all daisies and sunbeams.

Back in the shop, Liz would let me into a booth to listen to the latest hits, and I'd bop around, quite oblivious to the other shoppers. Later, as I dawdled back to number fifteen, smoking my first ever cigarettes, the music would still be in my ears, and I'd flick my feet like a dancer even if it was raining. I would feel like laughing, like blowing smoke rings. They were happy days indeed.

# Two

It was wonderfully peaceful to snuggle down in my bed at the end of the day, my work all done, my diary written and my prayers said. My sister, Ellen, had told me that if I stretched my arms and legs right down to my toes, I wouldn't be cold anymore. I'd relax and sleep deeply, as long as I had my teddy.

Hush – for a moment. But what was that? A creak on the stairs. I sat bolt upright. No one used these stairs but me. Perhaps it was Mrs Robertson needing something from me. Silence. I must have misheard. But no, another creak, and then suddenly a light under my door. The door handle turned.

'Hello? Who's...'

The shadow of his Lordship entered the room.

'Sir?' My voice was quiet, breathy. I flicked my lamp on as he put a finger to his lips, gently closing the door behind him. Before I could say another word he'd taken two strides and was at my bed. There was whiskey on his breath. His mouth twisted and he gazed down at me in wonder.

'Little good night kissy... Just a good night kissy, eh?' he slurred. I shrank and trembled, tugging my bed clothes up to my chest.

It all happened so fast. He reached over and put his fingers into my hair, pulling my head back, holding me in place.

'Sir, please,' I implored. 'It hurts... Please... I'm only sixteen... Sir, don't, you're frightening me... *Sir*...'

His eyes had a sightless look. His breathing was heavy. He wrapped his free arm around my waist and pulled me towards him. I struggled, kicking out, grasping at the headboard rail. He tugged at my nightie, tearing it suddenly over my head. My heart slammed into my mouth.

'No, no, no... Sir... Get *off* me!'

But against his strength I was hopeless.

8

His hands were all over my breasts, squeezing them, pulling them, wrenching them.

'Beautiful... Young... Tits...' He bit down on a nipple and sucked. 'Beautiful... Young...'

He slumped on top of me; the bed shifted under his weight. Then his hand was moving up my thigh. I felt his strong fingers sliding into me, parting me. The pain was sharp, excruciating.

'Cunt... Cunt... I knew you'd have a delicious cunt. I want... I want to... I want to fuck you... Lovely... Young... Cunt...'

Juddering movements into my tummy as he rammed his hips. *Please, God, let him stop. Please... Mummy...*

Suddenly his body convulsed, and he caught his breath. Then he froze and collapsed down on top of me. Sobbing, I scrambled away like a toddler, trying to pull down my nightie. Slowly he stood. Looking down at me, he shook his head.

'Fuckable,' he said. Then he moved slowly towards the door, sucking at his fingers. He stopped at the door, looking back. There was a dazed look in his oddly deep-set eyes. 'Oh, dear, don't do tears. Don't worry, it will be our little secret.' He fumbled with the door, then slammed it shut so hard behind him that my picture of St Francis of Assisi slipped from the nail in the wall and to the ground with a crash.

For a long while I lay there, very still and very empty.

My world might have collapsed like a pack of cards, but I still had to get up the next morning – still had to be dressed and down in the kitchen by seven o'clock, making the girls' boiled eggs and soldiers for their breakfast. And I was. But how to now pretend to be what I'd always been?

That morning, like any other, was all hustle and bustle. Two pairs of sparkling blue eyes gazed at me, the children giggling, noisy, seemingly intent on turning breakfast into a spoon-banging competition. I stood by the Aga waiting for the water to boil. Nanny Ford was busying herself in the larder, fetching the eggs, as the internal telephone rang. 'That'll be her, wanting her hot water and lemon,' I heard her muttering. 'Yes, my lady. No, my lady.' She sniffed, then took the call.

'Oh, good morning, your Lordship.' She glanced at me and grinned, her head cocked to one side. My heart skipped a beat. 'It's nanny, my lord... Yes, cook's gone off to see her sister... Just black tea and two rich tea biscuits? Of course, my lord... *The Sporting Life*? Very good, in a jiffy, sir.'

She hung up the phone. 'Right, my girl,' she said, looking at me, 'your legs are younger than mine. His Lordship wants his tea in bed. You know where the biscuits are kept. Just set a nice tray for him. Can't be feeling himself, not wanting a full English.'

I stood frozen to the spot, gripping the rail of the Aga, feeling my legs wouldn't hold me. One by one the eggs slipped from my fingers and onto the floor.

'Well, don't stand there gawping, Josephine, get a move on!' Not pausing for a beat, she shuffled over to quieten the children.

'I can't, nanny. I can't, please don't ask me.'

She stared at me, bewildered. 'No such word as "can't" in my book, young lady. What's come over you? You've not been yourself all morning. Have you got your monthly?'

'I can't... Nanny, please.'

She stared at me open mouthed. I groped for a tea towel to cover my face. If I was going to have to speak then let my shame not be seen and my words somehow be filtered.

In a voice hardly above a whisper, I told her what I could bear to repeat of my torment of the night before. She looked at me, her eyes wide.

'What are you telling me?' she said, and then, her face full of firmness, her voice gentle, she put her two hands on my shoulders. 'I'll take his tray up to him, dear, you look after the girls.' She grasped my hands with both of hers, her eyes suddenly alive, full of thought. 'I'll go and knock on Mrs Robertson's door. She'll have to attend to this. Oh, I'm sick to my stomach hearing all this filth.'

As she bustled out of the kitchen, I heard myself mumble, 'Sorry, nanny... Thank you, nanny.' Standing by the Aga, I could feel it in the walls. In my quavering soul I knew that my summertime in number fifteen, Kensington Square, was over.

# Three

Things turns out the way they're supposed to, I guess. But it was a swift slide from grace. As dusk fell that evening, the door of number fifteen slammed shut behind me with a thud. That door, that sound... I'll always associate it with the breaking of my heart. In my hand was a letter, signed by Mrs Robinson, thanking me for my all my hard work, but informing me that I was no longer required. Standing there, looking down the darkening street, my head drooped like a flower on a stem.

Falling, falling... Down I went, like Alice. But no magic awaited me. There was no Mad Hatter and certainly no tea party. All I wished for was to run home, that I'd never left... For all of this to go away. I longed to hear Mummy's voice, low, steady, soothing. I wanted to be alone with her, to spew out what I was feeling. The things I had done, had been forced to do.

But poor Daddy would have taken to his bed, Mummy enclosed herself in shame. Her innocent daughter violated. No, I told myself, I wouldn't, *couldn't* do that to them. I had to protect them. But if not to my parents, where could I turn?

Liz. That sweet girl, that strong soul, who said things like 'going with the flow', 'higher power', and 'aura'. I had no idea what she'd think of my misfortune. She always put a lot of stock in destiny. But she could make you laugh even through your tears, tears she shed with you, laughter she shared with you too. And besides, who else did I have?

The light was fading over Notting Hill Gate, dust and rubbish swirling from Portobello market, the early evening traffic noises unnerving me as my best black patent flatties beat the street.

I must have been walking for over an hour, my bag weighing on me heavier and heavier, by the time I at last found my way to Liz's front door.

I clung onto the door knocker. 'Please be home, Liz, please be home.'

I heard footsteps coming down the passage. Then there she was, in her flowered pyjama bottoms and white halter t-shirt, her hair wet from the shower.

'Oh, Liz, I'm in trouble…'

'Josephine!' She stepped forward, wrapping her arms around me and sweeping me inside. She led me to an armchair, where I scrunched up, drawing my knees up under my chin.

'C'mon,' she coaxed, her London accent, normally so broad, now soft as down. 'Talk to me.'

I was determined not to cry, and when I finally spoke, my voice came out low and controlled. But inside I was squirming, mortified at having to put the details of my abuse into words.

A look of horror passed across Liz's eyes. 'What a shit!' she interjected. She shook her head. 'Josephine, oh, Josephine… OK.' She put her cup down with a clatter. 'OK,' she repeated.

Then she was silent, and in the pause, a deathly chill spread over me. In my hurry across London, I must have been sweating, and now, in the cool of Liz's flat, the moisture was drying cold on my skin.

Eventually she spoke again, determinedly, looking into my eyes. 'This too shall pass. I'm here for you. Move in with me, we'll cope.'

I felt tears welling again. There were things that we'd need to discuss – details, practicalities. But not now, not now.

Liz busied herself making me a bed on the sofa. 'You look like a little bird who's fallen out of the nest,' she said as she shook out a blanket. 'Don't worry, little bird, glass of wine coming up!'

Later, as I snuggled down in my newly made up sofa bed, Liz's cats, Garbo and Brando, cuddling up to me, I made a promise to myself: one day my life would be golden. My abuse would not sour me; I would not live under that shadow. When I finally fell asleep, I dreamt of a wall of peeling paper. In the wall was a door. I was running towards it… Or was I running away?

I knew I would eventually have to face my parents, but it took me two whole days to work up the courage. Time to go back home. But what could I tell them? I knew it couldn't be the truth.

An empty tugging was in my stomach as I put my key in the lock. I tiptoed down the hall, Lady excitedly scraping her paws at my legs. 'Shhh, little love,' I whispered. I could smell the scents of my favourite dinner, chicken with roast potatoes and onion gravy.

Mummy turned as I entered. She was surprised to see me, and she studied my features intently. 'What is it?' she asked, putting her fork down. 'I can read you like a book.'

She and my father exchanged glances as he drained his glass.

I wish now that I had kept a note of all I said to them that evening. As I spoke I realised that everything I was saying was true, though some of it I had never even known myself until that moment. I had never dreamed of a life spent changing nappies, wiping babies' bottoms. There was no future in it. I could never return.

No, I told them, nannying was no life for me. I ached for the spotlight. Life was a game, a gamble, a toss of a coin, and I wanted to play for the big stakes.

In this way I danced on the edge of truth, spun them my yarn of white lies and evasions. But though they seemed wholly taken in, still I felt exposed, skimming over troubled waters like a seabird far from shore.

Mummy reached over and put a hand on my shoulder. Leaning over the table, her dark hair shimmering under the light, she fixed her eyes on mine. Then, frowning, she said softly, 'When you were a baby, you made our arms ache, and now you're older you make our hearts ache.' She turned to Daddy and smiled. 'I know I shouldn't be surprised. You always said she wanted to climb the rainbow.'

# Four

The wheels will turn – they always do. Christmas was only a few weeks away and the stores had been taking on extra staff. Liz worked her magic, charming her manager into offering me a job. She had called me 'little bird', and now she was taking me under her firm, protective wing. So there I was, selling Beatles and Stones 45s, looking over the covers as I accepted the proffered eight and four pence, and imagining my own name in lights.

After the hectic holiday period ended, I was asked to stay on. The manager, a Mr Laurenson, seemed to like me in a fatherly way, and would often bring me flowers from his garden. I was now earning just enough to be able to rent the bedsit next door to Liz. We still shared a kitchen and a bathroom, but I had my own space and she, bless her, had her privacy. I suppose it would seem I'd landed on my feet. But while I was truly grateful for everything Liz had done for me, there is not much to say about working in a record shop, and after seven months or so, my feet were itching to skip on to something new.

It was four in the afternoon, tea-break time in the back room of the shop. Sitting at the small lime Formica table, with its cigarette burns and coffee stains, I was smoking, thinking, watching the smoke as it twisted and arced. In my hand was a screwed up ball of paper, a cutting from *The Stage* magazine. It read: 'Wanted, young, vivacious, talented juveniles. Modelling and acting opportunities. Good terms and equity rates apply. Please call Barney Green of Top Talents and Associates, Paddington 2590.'

I took a deep breath, steeling myself, then got up and went outside. As I put a couple of coins into the slot of the phone box, I was so nervous my hands were shaking.

A man's voice answered, low and husky. 'Top Talent Associates here. Can I help you?'

'Mr Green, is that you?' I asked, feeling shy.

'This is he,' he said.

'Mr Green, er... I saw your ad in *The Stage* and I... My name is Josephine Cagney. Could I come and see you, please?'

' 'Ow old are you, my dear?' he asked.

'Eighteen,' I lied, feeling a bead of sweat trickling down my back.

'Well, we've 'ad a lot of calls, but come along to my office so I can take a look at you. D'you know Tottenham Court Road?'

It was agreed that I'd see him the next day. I thanked him politely, said goodbye, and left the booth flushed with excitement. That night I wrote only three words in my diary: 'Conceive. Believe. Achieve.'

The following morning, I walked up the steep stairs of the address I'd been given, up the worn carpet to the first floor, where the walls were lined with theatre posters. The door was ajar, but I knocked before entering. I found myself in a small room. Despite a large window, the smell of cigarettes was overwhelming.

Mr Green was a man of about forty. Small and gaunt, with a mop of greasy-looking dark hair falling across his forehead, he was wearing a shiny brown suit with a floppy red hanky in his breast pocket, and matching red socks slouching around his ankles. At the sight of me, he curled back his thin lips into what I supposed was a smile, showing his tannin-stained teeth. He stood and stepped around his desk. Catching my elbow with a slight upward pressure, he moved me to the other side of the room.

'Stand over 'ere, dear, against the wall. What's yer name again?'

He kept close. His breath smelled of brandy. He blew on his glasses, rubbed them and, replacing them, studied me with hard and glittering eyes. 'Tell me about yourself. Who are you?'

So, trying not to stutter, I told him.

I told him I was driven. Told him I wouldn't, *couldn't* just float around, accepting my life as it was. I wanted more. I'd start from the bottom rung. I knew I was pretty, knew I could sing and dance. I wanted a part of it, to *be* a part of it. *Show business*.

I maintained eye contact, trying to appear undaunted. I wanted him to know that this wasn't some fairy tale fixation, the dreams of some cosseted princess.

'Please take a chance on me, Mr Green,' I said. 'These aren't just words, I mean it. I want to start a new story, *my* story.'

15

My heart was crying out, *this is who I am*. In that moment I could see a glittering tomorrow. A tomorrow I could almost touch.

He stood there, looking at his shoes, his face unreadable. Of course, he had heard all of this before. He cleared his throat noisily, folded his arms and sat on the edge of his desk. 'Well, you 'ave a way with you, I'll give you that,' he said eventually.

I caught his eye and maintained eye contact, trying to appear undaunted.

'But d'you have more than ambition?' he continued. 'I see a dozen girls a week standing where you are, and all of 'em tell me they 'ave what it takes. And they bring headshots with 'em too.'

I blushed. It hadn't even occurred to me.

'How am I supposed to sell you if I don't know whether the camera likes you? There is a touch of a young Natalie Wood about you, though.' He coughed, sputtering up a gob of phlegm, which he swallowed again noisily. 'You still a virgin?'

The bluntness of his question threw me. Was I? Technically…

'Yes, of course.'

'You don't seem sure!'

'Yes, I am. I'm only eighteen!'

'Stand on the chair,' he said, pointing to a corner. 'Hitch up your skirt. Show me your legs.'

I did as I was told. I was trembling.

Silence. Then to my amazement, he burst into laughter. 'Josephine…'

My heart skipped a beat. 'Mr Green?'

'I'm crazy. Daft in the 'ead. I 'ave to be. Why you? Something special bout you, eh? Well then, why not? We'll give it our best shot. A trial – six months.'

'Oh my god! Oh my god!' I cried, feeling a peculiar weakness behind my knees as I leapt off the chair and went forward to hug him. His arms stayed hanging by his side, and he turned away from me, but I could see that he was smiling faintly.


Daddy had always said to me, you have to believe in happiness or happiness never will come. Luck is like love – you have to go all the way to find it. For an afternoon, I had forced myself to believe in my dreams. Now I had an agent! And through him a drama teacher, Iris Fleming.

I worked with Iris three times a week. I learnt so much from her, small, special touches that were the fruits of her long experience.

'You can't get to the truth through excess,' she'd say. 'The best actors can melt your heart with a single breath. Before a rehearsal you must whisper your way through the scene. Softly softly, Josephine, softly softly...'

I went to audition after audition, there were many aching humiliations, but Iris and Mr Green kept my hopes high, and I'd swallow my pride, put on my best smile and go again. Bigger and better things were ahead. Weren't they?

Months, years passed as days. In the record shop, my fellow shop girls would chatter about Mr Right, and I'd nod and smile, but words like 'settle down' disturbed me. Not for me, not yet. If it meant lonely days, lonely nights, then that was all there was to it. I determined to stay as unattached as tumbleweed. When my chance came, I would be free to take it.

# Five

Time will fly and truth will change. Me, a dancer in a Soho night club! How? I barely knew myself! It had been a whirlwind of auditions, phone calls, and a photo shoot where I pouted and struck poses to the direction of the photographer – and before I knew it, there I was, five months into my new life.

My time in the club had been good fun, of a kind. But I loathed the place itself. In the evenings it wasn't so bad, but in the dim daylight you saw the reality: grubby leatherette banquettes with traps for vermin hidden underneath them, scuffed walls stained by years of cigarette smoke. You could almost smell the seediness. The sunburst chandelier, meant to revolve above the giddy dancers like a glittering confection in a Busby Berkeley film, had fallen into disrepair. It was a place where middle aged men – 'Slippin' Jimmies', we called them – came to forget the reality of their lives, lounging, gawking, flashing their fat wallets and glistening cuff links, spending half drunken nights and a lot of cash to get a hard-on when the lights were low.

But there's either money in your purse or there isn't, and I refused to trouble Daddy for help. *Fuck 'em all,* I'd tell myself, as they leered up at me, *the short and the tall… They've no class, they can kiss my arse.*

The house band was made up of a pianist, a drummer and a bassist. I was one of a group of six girl dancers, and there was a lead girl who danced completely naked. On our heads, we had small towers of back-combed hair pieces; false eyelashes long and spindly as spider's legs; and scanty, semi-transparent, sparkly leotards under a layer of shimmering, silken gauze. On impossibly high-heeled shoes one size too small, I would try to glide my way around the stage.

We were experts at exchanging caustic remarks out of the corners of our ever-smiling mouths. 'Fuck me, look at that fat prick at table four. One for

18

you.'

'Oh thanks! I'd rather do my knitting!'

Later, alone in my rented room, I'd smoke the odd joint and stay up as late as I could. I'd drift off to sleep as the city slowly woke around me, my dreaming of darkened rooms and shadows of a deeper darkness moving in the corners.

It was in the late afternoon of my nineteenth birthday when I learned that our naked dancer, Kathy, had called in sick short notice. This was a problem. Kathy was the star spot of the show. Like the other girls, I was under no illusion that it was she who drew the punters. They loved her small, perfect body, and they certainly wouldn't be happy at her absence. A replacement had to be found among us. We were asked to draw straws. I drew the short one.

'Oh, please don't ask me. I can't show myself like that!' Instinctively I lifted both hands to cover my boobs, blushing and squirming like a child.

'Ooh, look at Miss Demure. Don't pull the shy little innocent on me. You'll get an extra fiver!' This was Stuart, the dance captain. He seemed to expect me to be thrilled at the opportunity. He was laughing; I couldn't even smile.

'I would feel so cheap,' I murmured.

Stuart ran his hands through his thinning grey hair, exasperated. 'Well, you shouldn't. You've a lovely body. The best tits and legs in the business. Don't forget to shave them, mind. Get out there tonight, show those silly old wankers what they haven't got at home.'

Leaning forward, he kissed the end of my nose. 'Don't worry, I'll look after you.'

He could be a vicious old queen, so was this a promise or a threat?

I gulped back a brandy as the centre stage lights dimmed to black and the band began to play my music, 'Come Fly with Me'. A couple of the other girls shoved me onstage, and the spotlight found me still trying to recover my balance.

I was being seen, watched. Dozens of leering eyes were directed at my body. I tried to be creative, pretending I was alone in my room, admiring myself in my long mirror. If I could just perform, act, I might make it through. I channeled the aloofness of Grace Kelly. It was just for this one night, just this one night. I pretended that Frank Sinatra was out front, ready to whisk me away to La La Land as soon the curtain fell.

But as I moved, I sensed the excitement from the audience. I felt my nipples stiffen. In turning them on could I be turned on too?

I could.

After that first night, I slipped into my pyjamas and toppled into bed exhausted. I switched off my bedside light and soon fell asleep cradling my crotch.

Kathy was ill for the next six nights, and each evening I stepped back onto the stage with yet more relish than before. The spotlight was like a magnet, and I was moving from the back of the line.

After my third evening, Morris, the little Jewish doorman, slipped a note into my hand. I shrugged and shoved it into the belt of my trousers. Envelopes were often left for me, some with sticky twenty pound notes folded inside. This one, however, contained a business card and an invitation to lunch the next day. Tiberio in Soho. One o'clock.

> *Simon Hastings*
> *Public Relations Consultant*
> *6 Cornford Gardens*
> *Knightsbridge*
> *London SW7*
> *Tel: Knightsbridge 3151*

You meet a lot of deadbeats on the club circuit; it's an occupational hazard. But Tiberio's! Trendy! Lots of Slippin' Jimmies. And a girl has to eat!

The next day, Simon Hastings was waiting for me at the bar, holding out a glass of pink champagne. Off to a positive start.

Tall and dark-haired with a touch of grey, lean-jawed and elegant, at a guess I would have said he was in his late thirties. A class act, which made a change.

'Good to meet you,' said Simon, circling a waiter to take my hand.

'Oh, thank you. Me too!' I giggled. 'I mean, to meet you.'

We took it from there. His listening was attentive, his conversation fluent. Without elaborating, he told me he was a literary agent. Divorced for the past two years, his ex-wife now in France. No acrimony, no children. No skeletons, as he put it.

Over frequent leisurely lunches in the following weeks, Simon learned

20

how it was I had come to work in such a dive. How it had all touched off a few years before when I was turned out onto the street aged just sixteen, with no reference, no wages, no chance. I shared what life had taught me. That emotional missiles could come out of nowhere. That happiness is never spontaneous. That there is no safe place for the tender hearted.

I had learned to live behind a mask, but being with Simon was causing it to slip. This was more than I'd ever shared. I wanted to talk about ambition, about how my life might one day be, well, beautiful. I made no secret of my wish for better things. I wanted to say that it was all within me, but was it? Or rather, wasn't that exactly my problem: that I talked the talk, but at the end of the day, that's all it was – talk, empty words? Was I at my best in my dreams? I told him I'd made a promise to myself that one day I would be somebody, and that I prayed every night that I would keep the promise.

It took a while for Simon to be as open with me. His questioning was relentless. 'I've got ears,' he joked. But when he did speak, I was impressed. He was so assured, and everything he said was suffused by his sunny good nature. It was a while before I broached the subject that had been foremost on my mind since our first meeting. Gingerly, I enquired as to why he was in the club that night, or any such club on any night, watching stark naked girls parade.

'I thought it odd you hadn't asked,' he said. 'I mean, what's a man like me doing in that horrible club, drinking that cheap champagne?' He laughed, raising his hands. 'I know how it must look, but I can explain.' He lit a cigarette. 'A client of mine is writing a book which takes place, partly, in a Soho strip club. He calls it research.' He snorted derisively, and I laughed along.

One afternoon after a long leisurely lunch, we walked slowly through the streets towards the club, holding hands. Apart from kisses on the cheek whenever we met, holding hands was our only physical contact. As we neared Old Compton Street, we stepped inside a doorway for him to light his cigarette. The smell of his cigarette seemed sweeter than any flower. I realized then that I was in big trouble. I wanted to be the cigarette in his mouth. I looked up into his espresso-coloured eyes. With a kind of dismayed surrender, I heard myself say, 'I'd rather just dance for you tonight.'

For an answer he puts an arm around my waist, holding me tightly to him. He picked up my hand and raised it to his lips.

I missed my rehearsal.

From Simon's bedroom I could hear the sounds of his rummaging through a drawer in his bathroom. Leaning by the door, I peeked my head round. 'I'm on the pill,' I said, my voice a soft whisper. He turned to me, stepped forward, pulled me into his arms. At first his kiss was gentle, and then his tongue reached up under my top lip and he started sucking hard on my tongue.

When he broke the kiss, his voice was husky. 'I want to fuck you and fuck you...'

I felt the tingling effect of those words quivering in the deepest, darkest part of me, sweet, sharp feelings that made me wet. My voice was breathy when I spoke. 'Me too, I want you inside me. Now.' Impatiently I bit down on his bottom lip.

He pulled back, his lips twitching with a hint of a smile. 'Naughty girl, so you like it rough.' Never breaking eye contact, he reached both his hands down. Cupping my backside and squeezing gently, he lifted me up, holding me against his hips. I felt his big, hard erection pressing against me, as he eased me towards his vast bed.

'Lift up your arms,' he said, his breathing ragged. I did as I was told, and he lifted my dress up and over my head, throwing it on the floor. Hooking his thumb into the waist of my black lace panties, he slowly slid them down my legs. Burying his face in them, he moaned gently. He moved his hand across my tummy in circular movements, moving them slowly up to my breasts.

Pulling my bra down, he gently squeezed and flicked my nipples with his fingers. His hands slipped down my body to my thighs. He pushed his fingers gently into me, setting up a rhythm. 'Oh, that's so...' I managed, closing my eyes.

He whispered a soft command. 'Keep looking at me, in my eyes, Josephine.'

He stood and quickly unzipped his trousers. Pulling his shirt and sweater over his head in one movement, he was back on top of me in a flash. He flipped me over onto my tummy. 'I'm going to take you from behind,' he whispered.

My hands reached up and gripped the bed head. Sliding his leg between mine, pushing them apart, he was suddenly inside me, his hands on my hips, holding me in place. I arched my bottom as he ground into me. Skin on skin, we moved together.

'Fuck me harder, harder,' I gasped.

All consuming sensations washed over me as he reached under me, fingering my clitoris. 'Let's go, baby,' he rasped.

We climaxed together like a blaze of light, my orgasm ripping through me like electricity, leaving my limbs trembling. Still entwined, his weight heavy on me, we slid off the end of the crumpled bed, and in the minutes that followed, we were quiet, the only sounds our thumping hearts and our gasping breath.

'Half time and orange juice?' I asked, my breathing short.

Groaning, he stood. '*Shhh*,' I whispered, 'the neighbours might hear. What'll they think?'

'Too late to think of that now,' said Simon, a smile creasing his face. 'Got to keep the soundtrack going.' He continued with his version of primal calls as he prepared us both drinks.

The next morning I woke to bright sunlight falling across the bedroom walls. Rising, I stood by the open window and read the wobbly-lettered note Simon had left for me by the phone.

'Ode to a delightful girl from a loving kind of guy. Was it all a dream? We need to talk about us. Josephine, can we be an us? Lunch at Don Lugies in the Kings Road Chelsea. One o'clock. Do we have a date? X.'

Standing very still, I could hear a blackbird trilling somewhere in the gardens below. Was he calling out to me? All the love songs, all the music of my mind seemed there in his song. Was I in love? You can't be prudent and in love at the same time. It took me a solid nanosecond for it to sink in: I *was*.

As if drawn by a magnetic force, I hurried to dress and left for Chelsea. The man I loved was waiting for me.

# Six

Iris Fleming wore a glittering diamond ring. A huge canary-coloured gemstone, its yellow eye stared optimistically at the world, and towards me. She encouraged me, made me believe that my fantasies could one day be a reality.

Like my father, perhaps her imagination was so powerful that once she had said a thing, she believed it to be so. She really believed I had a natural talent, and convinced of this, she became my mentor.

Rain slicked the cobbled street outside the windows that winter afternoon. I was in the apartment – *our* apartment, as I thought of it now, mine and Simon's – singing along to a new record, Dionne Warwick's 'Anyone Who Had a Heart', and wrapping Christmas presents. Just as the music ended, the telephone rang in the other room. In my haste, I tripped over a couple of boxes, picked up the receiver, dropped, recovered it and answered in as unflustered a tone as I could manage.

'Hello, Josephine?' It was Iris. At three pm the next afternoon she'd arranged an appointment with a hotshot movie producer, Jerry Grosfeld. 'I want you to be vivid, darling, at your very best. If he likes you he'll have you screen tested. It's a good part, there'll be lots of competition. The script is on its way. It's about a girl who says yes to life – perfect for you. This could be the one we've been waiting for.'

Then a click and silence.

The sky scowled with threatened snow as I hurried to The Dorchester Hotel. Mr Grosfeld was waiting for me in his small suite, which was light and spacious, with impressive views over Hyde Park and fancy wallpaper hung with Picasso prints. Mr Grosfeld was hardly a looker, the victim of a double receding chin, with insipid, bulging eyes and an inclination towards fat, but at over six feet tall, he was nevertheless a formidable figure.

He kindly cleared away a pile of newspapers so I could sink down into one of the squashy sofas.

There was a neat pile of black and white head shots on the coffee table in front of me. Mine was on the top, staring back at me.

He was effusive, almost spilling over with enthusiasm about his project. He was now on his feet, still talking, telling me about the director and his vision, and walking across to the bathroom. To my amazement, leaving the door wide open, he unzipped his trousers, allowing them to drop around his ankles, quickly followed by his underpants. Without a word of apology or explanation, he plonked himself down on the lavatory and continued the conversation. 'Michael York has agreed a deal... Sean Connery's playing hardball... Glenda Jackson has other commitments, but I'll keep at her...'

With the door still wide open and his seated figure in full view, looking out at me the whole time, I saw his saggy features strain. Then I heard a *plop*, followed by another: *plop plop plop*. I sat mute with embarrassment, mortified. At home Simon and I were close as close, but at such times the door to our bathroom was kept firmly closed. Some things are private. I'd seen – and heard – enough. Getting to my feet, I moved swiftly to the front door. One for the money, two for the show, three to get ready, and four to GO! Go *now!*

Simon arrived home that evening at around seven o'clock with a bottle of wine and a complete Chinese takeaway supper.

'How did your trip to The Dorchester go?' he asked.

I shrugged and reached up to ruffle his hair. 'It was... Exceptional,' I said, with a sharp little laugh.

And out it came. He rocked gently on his heels; then he burst into laughter so loud he had to stuff his clenched fist into his mouth.

'He did what?' he managed eventually, and insisted I tell him again, not missing out any detail or sound effect. 'Oh, darling, I think you need a drink.' Still chuckling, he started to dish out the takeaway. 'You sit back and take it easy.'

He was a darling of a man. I loved Simon. Simon loved me. We lived in a lovely part of London, and over time we'd made what had been his bachelor pad into a real home. How does the song go? There's no place like it. Home sweet home. I felt my cares falling from me like my clothes at the club.

Iris, as ever, was undaunted by my latest setback. She arranged for me to meet with a film director the next week. At the appointed time, I tapped on the door and entered into an office. There he was. This director, whose name is not to be mentioned, was standing by a desk, carefully tearing strips of newspaper then rolling them into a small twist and popping them into his mouth to suck on.

No chatter, just a limp hand shake and an 'Upstairs' – as if I was trash or less. He ushered me through an interior door and followed me up a short spiral staircase. I could sense he was looking up my apology of a skirt. A door opened out onto a grubby flat roof. 'Stand there, close to the wall,' he said. He held the camera only a couple of feet from my face. My agent had been vague, to say the least, as to what the part was: would it be 'Gritty Northern girl coming to London', or 'Chelsea daughter of bankrupt Earl' this time? Staring into the lens of the camera, I could almost believe it was for Mata Hari before the firing squad!

'More,' said the director, camera on shoulder as if it was a bazooka. 'More.' So I gave him 'more'.

'Less, much less.'

Then, abruptly, he lowered the camera. 'Do you have a boyfriend?' he said.

'Erm, yes. Yes, I do.'

'Well, get rid of him. I'm here to launch a new talent.' He put the camera aside on the brick wall. His right hand felt for the buttons on his fly. 'Now, Josephine, what can you do about this?'

Iris had warned me that there'd be days like this. Showbiz – that's just how it is. I didn't linger. I pushed past him and was downstairs in a flash.

They say bad things come in threes. Well, let me tell you, after what happened to me on the way home from *that* particular audition, I had my fingers crossed for the rest of the day.

I was stood, I well remember, sheltering from the lashing rain in the doorway of a large department store in Oxford Street. Umbrella, raincoat – I had neither. I was shivering, wet, and feeling thoroughly humiliated.

But then above the blustering elements, something reached me. Call it sixth sense, call it a premonition, call it what you will. *Something* made me look up, and just as I did so, time came to a standstill. Falling, falling as relaxed as a dead cat, a light brown, billowing shape. A bale of cloth, I thought, ridiculously. But then I made out a white disc attached to the front. In horror, I realised it was a face.

26

What is the sound of a body crashing, at terminal velocity, out of life and into death? Hitting the unforgiving surface of a London pavement from God knows how many storeys? *Crunch*? *Thump*? To this day, I couldn't tell you. But I can hear it still. The memory won't leave me alone.

My heart beat a crazed rhythm, my feet felt glued to the street. Terror overcame me, sheer shock, sheer confusion. Then I was thrown against a red letter box by a running policeman.

'Oh, he's finally done it, poor sod. Who's the girl? She's in a mess.'

What should have been inside the body of this tragic man was outside, over me. His limbs were twisted, broken, his head smashed into a bleeding mass.

'You've been lucky, miss. He nearly took you with him. Who can we call to come and get you?' I was rocking to and fro, my arms around the letter box; it seemed to be rocking with me. I heard myself making a peculiar noise, a strangled gurgling far back in my throat that bubbled into 'Mummy, Mummy!' Always Mummy. And then I fainted dead away.

What a difference a day makes! Much too early the next day the doorbell rang and a large package was delivered to our door. It contained a script. *The* script! A few weeks before I had auditioned for a part, and as Mr Green's enclosed note informed me, the director had loved me.

When Simon returned home I was waiting for him on the bed. Leaning on the doorframe, he met my gaze as I slowly began to unzip my knee high boots.

'I've had some good news,' I said, 'the best news, and I'm in the mood for celebrating.'

He was elegantly dressed as ever. Drawing deeply on a cigarette, he stepped towards me. Gazing upon this handsome man, *my* handsome man, with my big news still to share, I felt a sudden rush of joy, and I couldn't hold back any longer. As he raised himself onto the bed and leant over me, in one big rush I told him. I was going to be in a film, a real life film! Big budget, too, involving a six week shoot in Tunisia!

A moment of stunned silence.

'*What?*'

From heaven to hell in five seconds flat. Didn't I realise that this could threaten our relationship? What was he to do while I was off gallivanting around with my new film family? Had I given a thought to him at all? Now he had me pinned down on the bed, his face inches from mine, an acid-tinged reek of alcohol on his breath. I had a sudden flash of memory: the stench of gin on his Lordship's breath, his weight on top of me...

'You fucking actresses are all the same,' Simon yelled. 'Oh, look at you, the big star! Well enjoy it while it lasts, hotshot! Your use by date is on its way! You'll be old and alone, no one to fuck you. Well, I hope you'll be happy in your dank room in bloody Balham, nothing but a scrap book of your faded reviews and your dog eared newspaper cuttings, only a cat to keep you warm at night!' He brushed back his greying hair with an agitated hand. 'What a joke, all you had when I met you were two grubby bras and a toothbrush!'

I was stung by his spite. He had been used to me always putting him first. He'd felt safe, certain. He was shouting so loud, my ears ached. I was quaking. This onslaught of sneering and mockery – it seemed so unreal. Where was it coming from. All this bile – was it just the booze talking?

'You didn't think of me for a moment, you selfish bitch. You're a walking apology of a girlfriend!' His face was taut, scarlet with anger. 'You think you're the next Julie Christie. Is that what they tell you? These "friends" of yours, your film friends.'

Yes, I told him, that's what they said.

'Well, ho ho ho, ha ha ha, of course they do. Go on believing that one, honey. You'll find out for yourself soon enough.' A wild shine was in his eyes.

I begged to be heard out, to say my piece, to explain. I was sobbing, stumbling, choking over my words. 'It's my *job!*' I managed. 'It's what I *do*. We're not in *competition!* Why are you being such a... such a *pig?*'

'Fake, *fake*,' he sneered 'Save it for the paying punters.'

'So if we get married, you... You'd want me washing socks, ironing shirts? Is that it? Dinner on the table by six?'

I gazed up at him, a desperate plea in my eyes. With a wolfish sneer, he delivered the coup de grâce 'Marry *you?* Oh darling, that was never on the cards. You were just the best bang for my buck. You with your clockwork cunt. I only wanted you as a fuck thing.'

And with that, he was gone: out the front door, down the stairs and gone. I slumped down to the floor, feeling like I'd danced with the devil himself. How could I have been so blind?

I heard the car starting, then pulling away. I suddenly felt a long way from home: lost, marooned with no hope of rescue. I pulled my pillow from my bed, and pressed it to my face. Think of nothing, think of icy water.

A few months previously, I had auditioned for a play, an adaptation of story by Tennessee Williams. I hadn't got the part, but there was a line that had stuck with me:

'There is a great danger to such a love. When the loved one is lost, the life is lost. It crumbles to pieces.'

My love for Simon was the core of my life. Show Simon this, tell Simon that, buy for Simon...

Crumble to pieces? Oh, please. Not my life. Not me. I'm a scheming, dreaming Scorpio female. I'll make a go of it, don't you doubt. To succeed is a neat form of revenge. He doesn't get to win.

# Seven

I was bruised beyond belief. But I had something to break my fall: *Desert Interlude*, my first acting role. Out of the shadows and into the spotlight! Look at me Daddy, watch me go… I was headed for Tunsia. Nothing could touch me, nobody could dim my excitement. My life was going to change, I could feel it. Back in my so called 'dank room in bloody Balham', I'd thrown myself into the script, and I knew it now like the back of my hand. I was ready, and I was leaving tomorrow.

Simon might not have shared my happiness, but at least my family had. I'd called by for dinner the previous evening, and as Mummy had fussed with concern, asking me how I was, how I was coping with the break up, I had announced, 'I'm happy as can be. I'm on my way.'

'Ooh, she's going to be a celebrity, can I have your autograph?' Johnny teased.

Daddy had uncorked some wine, and after pouring four glasses of ruby red, he proposed a toast. 'To Josephine, may she shine and sparkle, but stay forever sweet.'

We had raised our glasses, and tearfully, I had said, 'Oh, Daddy, I won't change, I promise.'

My daddy had smiled, but in his eyes I could see a kind of sadness, and when he spoke his voice was low. 'No, darling, but we'll have to.'

It was the last day in January. The winter had been ceaselessly wet, but that day London had its best face on, as if to give me something to remember it by while I was on my travels. I was wearing my St Christopher medal and brimming with all the optimism of youth.

I met up with the cast and crew at the airport, and Alberto, our director, introduced himself to all of us. A droopy eyed man, as he passed me, he stroked my bare arm with the back of his hand, the strap of my summer dress catching on his little finger. 'Ah, bella, the fair skin of the English,' he schmoozed.

I pushed the strap of my dress back onto my shoulder. 'Grazie,' I said.

'Listen to me, Bella Josephine,' he whispered, 'the camera has a cruel lens, but I will show you how to sparkle on the screen, to light it up.' Before he passed me to greet the rest of the crew, his hand lingered on my arm again.

The next day I found myself in the streets of a medieval fortified coastal town. I walked through the hot streets, enjoying the smells of the herbs, the spices, the baskets of lavender, cardamom, ginger, dates and fish. The central market square rang with the sounds of energetic trading. I soaked it all up, stopping to sample cups of mint tea, the delicious hot pastries filled with local cheese, nuts and spinach. *Click click click* went my camera, but how could I capture all this atmosphere on film?

The Arabian architecture and white washed riads under a sky the colour of opals, my birth stone. The call to prayer resounding across from a minaret. In my mind I was out and away, on a magical flying carpet ride. It took me to a souk where I bought strange leather slippers with turned up toes, a basket of dried rose petals and exotic bath oils, and a white cotton bath robe for my mother with a hood with a red tassel. It took me to a café where the owner chuckled away as I inhaled from a hookah pipe. The locals were so open and friendly, with a smile and a welcome for everyone.

But as it was getting dark, and I was walking back to the hotel, I had to pass close to the port. As I stopped to figure out my way, from an open doorway came a whisper. 'You want big cock, lady? Make you happy for two shillings?'

'Yuk, not me!' I replied emphatically, with a snort of derision. I wheeled away, scuttling helter skelter down the shiny cobbles, damp from a shower. This episode was not to be mentioned in my letters home.

The following morning, with huge excitement and a thumping heart, I pushed open the solid soundproof doors and stepped onto stage two. It was a vast, noisy space bustling with people concentrating on the job at hand. Carpenters banging, tracks being laid, booms being tested... There were voices calling out to one another in so many different languages. I barely understood a word.

But I had my own job to do. My first film role, and I would be appearing opposite the world famous Luisa Loquasto. I'd read so much about her, seen her staring back at me from the cover of so many glossy magazines. And today I was to meet her! I'd studied my lines long into the night; I could have reeled them off backwards. Now, in full makeup and costume, I was ready.

Alberto spotted me from across the stage and beckoned me over to him. He took hold of my hand and squeezed it hard. His voice, always thick with his native accent, rang with positivity. 'We are just setting up, not ready to go just yet. You must meet Luisa.'

There she was! Sitting in a green canvas chair alongside her assistant, she beckoned me to join her. Her dark lashes fluttering, she turned the full beam of her eyes, those famously mesmerising emeralds, towards me. 'Don't they feed you in London?' she asked, without removing her cigarette from between her lips. 'Well, little girl from London, you must show us what you can do.' With a slender ivory hand she firmly squashed her cigarette into a dish, and standing, she nodded for me to follow her. Alberto watched us from his chair next to the camera. He reminded me of a beached seal.

There are missed opportunities and seized opportunities. I was going to seize this one. I knew that my character needed size, impact. And while I might have been slight of body, I was sure that this was my part. I felt I knew this girl. Nobody else could play her.

But I hadn't counted on Loquasto. The rehearsal began, I hit all my marks, reeled off all my lines, but she worked the scene in complete isolation. She seemed barely there, like a ghost drifting through mist. Expressionless. Never looking towards me, mumbling her lines, moving with a deathly slowness from one end of the set to another. Picking up a prop, putting it down. Picking up another just to place it down exactly where it was. It was like she was in a trance.

I had worked so hard on the script, but without any response from her, all my timings, my rhythm, collapsed. I could only gulp my way through my lines without any conviction whatsoever. I was completely thrown, humiliated at her seeming indifference to me. Acting is like a game of ping pong. You serve, they receive; they serve, you receive. And you listen to each other. Loquasto, it would seem, didn't want to listen to me – didn't want to hear me, didn't want me there.

During the third read through, I noticed some of the crew had their eyes lowered. There was a lot of shuffling of feet, shared looks of embarrassment, a few heads shaking. This was not what I'd been hoping for. All my hard work just for some up-her-own arse star to have a strop. A change, like a shift of wind, came over me. Right then, bitch, knickers to you, I'll go to town.

I turned in a performance that Bette Davis would have been proud of. I was relentless, and at the end of the scene, all my anger spent, I heard a small ripple of applause from the crew. Alberto called for a brief break, and before he had even finished speaking, Luisa was off, without even a word for me, barracking her assistant in Italian.

I was having a chat with one of the producers when Alberto appeared at my shoulder. Putting his hand on the small of my back, he guided me peremptorily towards my dressing room.

When we were in private, for once he seemed lost for words. He was avoiding my gaze, and when he did finally speak, his voice was shaky. Luisa Loquasto had somehow taken me as a threat. He threw up his hands. 'Complicato!' he exclaimed. 'Luisa, she wants Susannah York, Luisa, she is the money...'

Scowling, he gabbled away, wringing his hands and shaking his head, and before I had at all recovered, he was out of the door, heading back towards his office.

So I was off the picture. What a frail ally Alberto had proven. I'd thought he might put up some opposition. Boy, was that a mistake.

Assume nothing.

Oh, how dark was that night, dark as blackberry juice, no moon, no stars, and darker still my heart.

# Eight

The click of the letter box told me the postman had been. Amongst the clutter of junk mail, I saw one fresh white envelope. My heart lifted as I read the address on the back, which told me it was from my agent. I swiped it up from the mat and had to hold back from waving it around triumphantly. As I tore it open, a cheque for nine shillings and six pence fluttered to the floor, and in that second has my ego ballooned – only to then burst into shreds as I read the letter also enclosed.

*Dear Josephine.*

*Your attitude on the set of Desert Interlude was not what we expect from one of our clients.*

*Luisa Loquasto is a world star. Treating her as less than such is more than arrogant, more than disappointing. We went out on a limb to get you this casting, and you repaid our trust by getting yourself fired. As such, this agency must, as they say in the States, let you go.*

*I would say good luck in your future career, but I'm not sure further encouragement is in your best interests, unless you give serious thought to your attitude. I am bitterly disappointed. I thought you might be one of my fledglings who would fly.*

*With regret,*
*Barney Green*

I was on a ship that had run aground, leaving me staring out of a window at unreachable horizons. Fuck it, *fuck it*. He can't do this to me! Oh, but he can and he has. I did nothing all day but hang around near the phone, which, like a kettle, will never do a thing while you're staring at it. I was conscious of time fleeting by. I wanted to live, to lose myself in, the world of acting, the world of illusion, of sudden hope and swift reversals. Of expansive love and revenging hate. I wasn't ready to accept anonymity. And I certainly wasn't prepared to let my dreams be killed by a letter. A sirocco had blown against me, but all storms pass. The bough might bend, but it doesn't break. I was still standing. Pausing only to grab an umbrella, I headed straight out the door.

I am a Londoner. Clogged and congested it may be, but the city is in my very spirit. In those years it seemed that the whole world had come to the capital. There, the best Greek and Indian restaurants, the first taste of the world to come. The streets thronged with the young, the exotic, the new, as London shrugged off the shadows of war and stepped into the bright new day.

I'd sit for hours in the window of Pechon, a perfect French patisserie in Queensway. This was my club, with its Victorian double-fronted windows, its air of faded grandeur, the hustle and bustle of regulars and tourists coming and going on the day's changing tide. I'd eat meringues so yummy I could never stop at one, and devour round cushions of white bread dusted with flour. It was there that I first met Victor, and our lunches very soon became tradition.

Victor was around forty-seven, a gay Harley Street physiotherapist. 'You're the Prince of Bayswater!' I'd tease him. He was always dressed to the nines: Savile Row suits, preferably in the colours of dark grey or black, with perfect Turnbull and Asser shirts, and always a spotted silk handkerchief flopping from his breast pocket. He kept his dark thinning hair hidden beneath a black fedora; on the rare occasions he would remove it, you'd see his forehead freckled by too many Barbados holidays with his friends Ronnie and Misty. 'I fried myself, darling!' he'd squawk, going on to explain how he'd rubbed in olive oil and vinegar as a sun cream. He wore glasses with red frames over eyes the colour of a trout's belly, a heavy antique gold ring set with diamonds, and on his left wrist a large oval Cartier watch. Always with a small stick pin of blue forget-me-not set in enamel with minute diamonds on his lapel. It had been a gift to his grandfather, Charles, from the Duke of Norfolk, to whom he'd been valet way back when.

One morning he came over, blowing a kiss and hooking his Gucci shoulder bag on the back of his chair. 'Salut, darling!' he boomed, sitting down opposite me. 'How's Bayswater's answer to Natalie Wood?'

I shushed him, telling him not to be so silly, but Victor didn't do restrained. He continued breezily, 'I'll be able to say I knew her when she had holes in her knickers!' A sudden hush in the coffee shop. 'Where were you last night then? You were missed!'

I didn't know where to start. 'Oh, I stayed in. I've been feeling... I mean, I'm feeling rather dreary today, sorry.'

He picked up his cup and drank his coffee. I avoided looking at him, although he was trying to catch my eye. All this evasion can be very irritating for the person on the receiving end. But not Victor. Sweet and attentive as ever, my caring friend coaxed me gently, and eventually out it spilled. My fears and worries – my conviction that my dreams were drifting ever further from my reach. I told him all, holding nothing back.

'Well, what are you going to do about it?' he said cheerily, once I had finished.

'I don't know.'

'What else *can* you do?'

'I'm an actress, that's what I can do. Other than that, not much.'

'Can you type?' he said with sudden enthusiasm.

'Just about – with two fingers maybe.'

'Well, I'll call Noel Davis then,' he said. 'He's a patient of mine. He wiped chocolate from his lips. 'He owes me.'

'Why call him?' I asked, taken aback.

'Because you need to get back on your feet, my girl. Truthfully, Josephine, you need a job. A proper job,' he added shortly. 'Noel has a very busy casting office – very connected. You could help around the place. The work would be pretty menial, of course, but you'd be able to hear the latest buzz of the business. He's friends with *everybody* who's *anybody*. You'd still feel sort of, well, involved... In the running. I know the dancing keeps you in pocket money, but you've got bills to pay.'

'Don't rub my nose in it,' I snapped despite myself. 'You think I don't know? You think I can sleep at night for worrying? He was right, of course. Work at the club had slowed, the tips of the punters now going into the pockets (or lack thereof) of a buxom brunette newcomer called Mimi. My friends, even my family had been happy to lend me money to tide me over, but I knew I'd used up most of my credit.

So the next morning I called the number Victor had given me, and over the next few days an arrangement was hashed out. I was to work in Noel's office, as a general dogsbody, on trial for a month.

Noel, sitting in his large leather chair from which he seldom moved, presided over his busy office with a calm but ruthless professionalism. His manner was quiet and stern. But he had a kind face and was generous with his help to me.

And so the merry-go-round geared up. I'm here, there, everywhere, at everyone's beck and call. 'Josephine, can you find...' 'Josephine, will you fetch...' Josephine, will you call...' 'Josephine will you make...' It was exhausting, but I kept my head down and my nose clean, and tried not to cause a stir. The only thing I made a face at was being asked to clean the loos; I turned a stone-deaf ear to that one.

In my first week, there was only one hiccup, when I bumped into Fred Zimmermann on the stairs. 'Good Morning, Mr Hitchcock,' I said brightly.

Looking at me over his rimless half glasses, he raised his hand in mock shock. 'He is much fatter than me!' Oh, blimey! I would have to do better than that.

Midway through my third week, I was standing laden with heavy scripts to be taken to the post office, reaching to press the button for the lift. The doors slid open before me, and I stood aside to let the occupant, a man I had never seen before, pass. He smiled at me. 'Those look heavy, let me hold the gate back.'

'Are you looking for Noel Davis?' I asked. 'If it's Steve Kenis at William Morris, he's on the next floor.'

'Don't worry,' he said, grinning. 'I know where I'm going.' He cocked his head. 'But where are *you* going?'

'The post office,' I said, slipping into the lift, smiling my thanks. He didn't move, just remained holding the door open, looking at me. Then with one step he was in the small lift with me, pulling at the handle to descend. It was a bit squashed in there with the two of us; we had to stand very close together.

'Here, let me,' he said, reaching to take the packages off me. He was looking at me with such amusement that my face flushed. 'I haven't seen you around before. Where has Noel been hiding you?'

'I'm the new girl in town,' I told him. 'I haven't been here a month yet.'

He looked at the packages he was now holding; the note on top read: 'Josephine – take to post office.'

'Hello, Josephine,' he said, smiling. 'My name's Steve. Not so fancy as Josephine, but an easy one to remember!'

As the lift stopped, he reached over and slid the gate open. Looking me straight in the eyes, he said, 'Let's do this,' shifting the packages from one arm to another. He touched my back for me to go first and followed me out into the lobby.

As we left the post office, light thunder rolled through the air, and it began to spot with rain. Steve jerked his thumb at the darkening skies. 'It would be a shame to bring you back bedraggled. What do you say you join me for a cup of coffee.

'I'd love to, Steve, but I have to get back to the office.'

With a mock sigh he fixed his eyes on me. 'I don't like drinking champagne alone.'

My faint protest ended there.

After a few minutes of relaxed preliminaries about British films and British weather, of which he amusingly approved, he amiably told me he'd been born in Austria, and as a little boy had escaped with his family to America before the German invasion. He loved California, had a home there as well as here, he was a director and writer, and his dream was to make a Western of Hamlet. He was off to Paris the next morning to pitch the idea to Sam Spiegel. 'Out with my begging bowl,' he said with a laugh.

He seemed to have a thirst to share; I didn't have to smoke him out, and I lapped it up. His voice was smooth, and only once did it drop, his eyes shifting from mine. 'By the way,' he interjected awkwardly, 'I'm married.'

I received this without flinching.

'Her name is Carol.' His eyes dropped. 'She can't travel with me anymore. She's suffering with MS.'

Why didn't I leave right then? Of course I should have. Ran away, from myself as much as him. But reality comes like rain after a drought; it isn't reasoned out of thin air.

Instead, scarcely audible, all I managed was: 'Poor her. Poor you . I'm so sorry.'

Heaven help me, over two champagnes and a shared slice of lemon meringue pie, I'd fallen in love. And when, a few days later, I received a telegram, I felt a thrill right down to my bones.

'Hello, Josephine,' it read. 'It's a holiday weekend. Let me show you Paris. You said you hadn't been here. Please join me. Ticket waiting for you at the Heathrow BA flight desk. Room booked for you at the San Simon Hotel. I shall be deeply sad if I don't see you. Tell me yes, this minute. Steve.'

I held the thin piece of paper tight – read it again, my lips forming each word, my heart going crazy, my face hot. *Here it comes,* I thought. *I'm in trouble. He's married. He's* married…

But of course I went. For ever after, I have dated events in my life as having happened before or after Steve.

# Nine

M y first visit to Paris! I already had a detailed mental picture of the city, so often photographed, painted, dreamed of. April in Paris, chestnuts in blossom, holiday tables under the trees… But there is so much more to the city of lights than any song lyric could ever suggest. Besieged, invaded, occupied, and now stepping elegantly into the new world, magical, aphrodisiacal Paris!

I'd slipped into the San Simon Hotel bar, and Steve was there waiting for me with a glass of champagne.

'Here you are.'

'Here I am.'

He was dressed a touch on the Italian side, in fine dark linen, with a crisp, white, open-necked shirt, dark loafer shoes and no socks. We were both of us beaming at seeing each other again. I knew, then, that this one was going to be altogether different. The big wipe out of all relationships that had gone before. Fooling around was over.

But as he wrapped his arms around me, I felt a twinge. He was married, a married man. But what is there to say about falling in love? It knows no restraint. It is selfish, selfish, but oh so sweet…

So, there I was, sipping champagne with this theatrically handsome gentleman, my heart skipping beats, lost in the moment. Was the magic of the city to blame?

'Let's go for a walk,' he said, offering me his hand.

He led me to Tuileries Garden, where we walked and talked, the gravel of the pathways crunching under our feet. Steve did much of the talking. At one point he stopped in front of me, wrapping an arm around my waist.

'If you want wedding bells and white doves, Josephine, I can't promise you that,' he said wearily. 'I'll never leave her. Not with her… condition.'

He pressed his finger tips against his temple and shut his eyes. What could I say? I waited for him to continue. 'Jesus,' he said eventually. 'Jesus, Josephine. I want to give you everything you want, everything you need... Everything I have, it's yours. Take it, if you want it. But I can never, *never* leave her.'

A flock of starlings flew across the sky, looking for somewhere to roost, and it seemed to me their wing-beats spread a nervousness through the park. I couldn't think of anything to say; I didn't know where to start. So instead I reached for Steve's face and kissed his closed eyes, his forehead and his lips. He kissed me back softly. Then he squared his shoulders. It was like he was tired of carrying them around.

After supper at de Crillon we walked back to our hotel. It was one of those evenings that darkened through all the imaginable shades of blue. We walked through the now darkened foyer, his arm across my shoulder. 'Shall we go to your room?' he asked.

'Yes.'

We fell into each other's arms. It felt like... home. Our beating hearts. Home.

'I want you,' came his soft, insistent groan. There was a faint flush on his cheeks and his eyes were half closed. Wordlessly, I led him upstairs.

We stayed there until dawn, sharing the sunrise. Love, oh love, I know now what you are.

Next morning, swimming in our happiness, we walked through the park wearing no overcoats, enjoying the sharp breeze. In Deux Margot, – 'my favourite café,' as Steve informed me – he was greeted warmly by the staff, who called him 'Monsieur Steve!' An almond croissant for me, crusty white bread for him, and thick black coffee stronger than anything I'd ever had in England. It was only mid-morning, but the cafe was already busy, and the air was acrid with cigarette smoke.

We were sitting close to an American man. He wore a plaid poplin sports jacket and a blue baseball cap. Red-faced, chewing on his crispy toast, the man beckoned to a waiter. 'Garçon,' he slurred, 'monsieur, sieve au please, avec... more bootere?' I thought for a moment he was kidding. We sat there in an agonized mixture of amusement and embarrassment.

The waiter shrugged and asking him with a strained grin, 'Beurre, monsieur?'

As we left, the lady at the pay desk, recognising Steve, beamed at him, chatting away familiarly. I understood just enough to know she was talking about one of his films. The French are crazy about film. She seemed dazzled by him. It was to be a while before I could accept that celebrity is a completely different world. I have always been an observer; it's important if you are an actor. Now in a world new to me, in France, by Steve's side, wherever we went I was aware we were the ones being observed.

Back in my empty flat, I plopped myself down on my bed and laced my fingers behind my head. 'Oh this is lovely,' I said, out loud, luxuriating in my solitude, where I could indulge myself in thoughts of Steve, of Paris. The clear spring sunshine shone through the open window. It was peaceful, quiet. I suppose I had been searching for a long time for someone to love, to put first. If it weren't for the pricking of my conscience every time I thought of Carol, I could have believed my world in that moment was perfect.

A few nights later, I had supper with Liz.

'Josephine, don't you ever feel lonely?' she asked me wistfully.

'Sometimes, but only lonely for him.'

Pacing like a cat up and down her small kitchen, she persisted. 'Don't you want to be married?'

'Not an option,' I said emphatically.

It was the price I had to pay – it was my choice. There was no one to whom I might turn; my parents, my friends, they would all be scandalised by my actions. A married man with a sick wife… I could hear them now: 'Don't you have any sense of decency, Josephine.' I shut out the voices. Don't go there.

Here in my flat, in the heart of the hustle and chaos of the city, I could block the world's censure from my mind. But I knew I was living a fantasy, a dream. But when I slept at night, the dreams of my slumber were not those of my waking. They were feverish, twisted.

It was indeed a new life, if not a new world. I had no plan, no thoughts other than of Steve. The taste of him, the feel of him; the sound of his voice; his intellect and quick wit. When we were together, I felt complete. This was peace. This was happiness. If we were meeting that evening, I'd be elated all day. A holiday feeling. The feeling of being high.

He'd leave the studio early, stop off at a florist and the off-licence, and we'd spend the evening wrapped in each other's arms. As dawn broke, with a surreptitious look at his watch, he'd reach over for the small gold ring on the bedstead, replacing it on the fourth finger of his left hand. Sitting up and

41

stretching, and after making me comfortable with my pillows, he'd whisper, 'I'm sorry to leave you.'

And then I would be left alone with only the hope my flowers might not fade before he returned. Man of my heart, Steve... Steve. Loving a married man is a bit like assembling an old jigsaw: no one has all the pieces. If tears came to my eyes when I had these thoughts, I let the hot drops fall.

# Ten

The next morning I went to Pechon, sat down opposite Victor at our usual table, and ordered a pain au chocolat. 'I have so much to tell you!' I blurted, and sparing him only the intimate details, I shared with him the story of my new life, my new love.

He listened with a faraway smile, but his eyes lacked their usual twinkle, and he kept shifting around on his seat.' This is crazy,' he said, eventually. His eyes seemed like small black holes. 'Josephine,' he continued, 'you are thinking with your cunt.'

*Christ*, I thought, *it gets better*. I lit a cigarette, inhaling deeply to steady myself.

'What about work?' Victor persisted. 'Hello, show business calling, anybody home? You have talent, and it's a crime to waste it. One disastrous experience and you throw in the fucking towel? I'm not impressed, my girl, not at all.' His tone was one usually reserved for children. 'Get back out there, show this so called Mr Wonderful that there is so much more to you.' Then softly, through gritted teeth, he delivered the coup de grâce: 'Your parents gave up so much to give you opportunities – opportunities you are now wasting. Wake up!'

He could go on till closing time, but there was no need. I felt like I'd been totally rumbled. He was right, of course, and his warning had come not a day too soon.

I caught his eye and he fixed me with a steely gaze. After a short moment, I giggled. 'You do sometimes get het up for a tubby old queen.'

By the time we were making to leave, we were the best of friends again. 'Goodbye, darling,' he said, blowing me a kiss as he swished from the café and into his day.

I grabbed my raincoat and ran lickety-split back to the office. My feet pounded the pavement, my hair steamed; I splashed my way through the puddles with a feeling of exhilaration.

As I burst into the office, Noel looked up from his reading. 'Josephine, Christ, you look a fright. Get out of that raincoat and into a dry martini. Billy Wilder coined that one, you know. So witty, so talented. And talking of talented directors, how's "le affair" going?'

I was stunned. 'How did you...?'

'Casting Queens know everything, Josephine.'

I found my voice to tell him what Victor had said. After a pause, Noel smiled. 'Well, we didn't think you'd last long behind the Olivetti. And as you know, we are casting this Schlesinger thing down in Dorset. If John likes you, there might be a cameo in it for you. Sometimes it only takes one good scene to get the ball rolling, you know.'

I had never seen a house with a cinema before. But there I was, the secretary introducing me, as the brightly lit room shone, unflatteringly, on John Schlesinger's bald dome. One of cinema's most enigmatic directors, he was completely charming, putting me at ease immediately, chatting away, asking me about myself, my journey, and discussing views from the papers he had been reading.

But then came the moment I had been dreading. 'Can you improvise?' asked the great man, crumpling a paper and tossing it over to me. I managed to catch it. 'It's a bird,' he told me.

I peeled the paper gently apart to reveal my imaginary black bird. I stroked it, cooed to it, held it aloft and set it free. Another squashed ball of newspaper came my way. This time I imagined it was a birthday cake, candles and all. Having feigned surprise and pleasure, I puffed and blew them out. Job done, I felt. Not at all. He sent me yet another scrunched up newspaper ball to play with. I screwed the newspaper into a squiggly shape and imagined a pistol. I polished it, made sure it had bullets, and having taken careful aim, fired it straight at him. 'Ow!' he screamed, his blue eyes glittering as he slumped, moaning into one of the seats.

I felt like it was going well. But there is always a moment when I just have to put my size fives into it. Out of the blue, I asked, 'Where's your wife this evening?'

John studied me suspiciously. 'He's at the ballet.'

But then he cracked into a smile, and we both started to laugh. Laughing with John Schlesinger! A moment to savour.

# Eleven

'What?' I shrilled, clinging to the phone.
'Yes, the part's yours,' Kenneth's voice crackled. 'He loved you.'
I thought his tone a touch sarcastic.

'Seems to think you're refreshingly eccentric,' he continued, expounding on the details of the offer. Then he hung up.

Kenneth was to be my new agent. Noel had recommended him to me, and me to him. It was fair to say that Kenneth wasn't cock-a-hoop at the idea. But at Noel's insistence, he had begrudgingly accepted.

Alone in my room, I shrieked maniacally, almost blowing kisses down the phone with excitement. My breath came no more than a thimbleful at a time. The great John Schlesinger wanted *me!* Thought I was gifted!

Eight days later I was on the night train gliding its way to Dorset. I was so happy, the stars seemed to sing in the sky above me.

About an hour after I'd arrived at the unit's hotel, I received a brief telegram from Steve. 'Darling girl,' it read, 'a day without you is a day without sunshine.' I kissed it lightly before hurriedly stuffing it away in my purse.

I was focused. I recognised the feeling, a little roll… a thrill, not in my tummy, not inside me at all – an external thrill that existed out there, in the air, radiating its energy on me, waiting for me to grasp it. I cosied myself down into my chair with the script in my lap, and for the next four hours I lost myself in it.

Eventually I must have dozed off, as I was still in my chair when dawn broke and there came a knock on the door. 'Miss Cagney,' came Ian, the third assistant's nasal voice, 'your car is here to take you out to the location.'

I jumped to my feet, and in five minutes my teeth were brushed, my hair combed, and I was out the door and, hey-jiggity-jig, on my way.

Like all the best directors, Schlesinger didn't believe in telling an actor what to do. All he would say, and only ever in the softest of voices, would be what *not* to do. Although challenging, he was kindly, always approachable and open to suggestion.

My part wasn't huge in terms of dialogue, but I was in most scenes, and I was needed almost every day. Dawn calls, long hours – it was bliss. Rain or shine, Dorset was beautiful that spring, and Schlesinger was all optimism, enthusiasm and control. Any anxieties he might have had about the tight schedule, he kept to himself.

A film set is like a beehive: everyone has a job to do. The costume designer with their Polaroid camera; the assistant directors with their call sheets; the continuity girl with her script and stopwatch; the camera crew; the sound crew waiting for an aeroplane to ruin a take... For an actor, the most important crew members are the costume, hair and makeup departments; tight knit and protective, they thought of us artists as their charges. It was like having several mummies.

When the credits roll at the pictures, by the time you are probably on your way to catch the last bus home, they, all the essential people, receive their moment in the sun, at the bottom of the roller.

Although the film was set in the eighteenth century, my character wasn't that far removed from me. I was playing the younger sister of the main female, all tight corsets and bouncing curls.

There was a lot of standing around in fields and at sea shores, huddled in groups shivering while Nick Roeg, the cameraman, searched for the sun. We had plastic rain hats to protect our wigs, thermal long johns and squeaking Wellington boots concealed under fluffy flounces, but we were ever on the alert, ready to shoot when the call came. 'Action, darlings!'

Underneath the banter, we were always ready. You have to be. The camera never lies. Whoever you were to be that day – an ingénue, a tormented soul, a sexual predator – you had to keep them living inside you, ready to jump forward, out of your skin and into the world. At the drop of a hat you had to step forward and *be* them in the moment.

Even if Steve had been in England, he would never have stepped onto another director's set – it was an unwritten rule not to do so. So apart from the daily bunches of flowers he so thoughtfully sent me, we were in different worlds. I missed him, of course, but my dedication was intense. As Noel said,

'I'd left the dreaded Olivetti' and thank God too!

One morning on set, while we sat listlessly in our canvas chairs, gossiping and trading old jokes, our leading actor, a man with the face of an angel but who could politely have been called vertically challenged, turned to me. 'Last night,' he said, 'I walked up and down outside your room, wondering if I should come in.' He ran a hand down one of his muscular thighs.

With an astonished gasp, I informed him that I had a boyfriend. 'So?' he clucked, smoothing his thigh again. 'What happens on location stays on location.'

I was greatly relieved to hear my name called. 'Josephine, on set please, we're ready for you.' I wouldn't, *couldn't* play his game. Like a fart in the wind, I was gone, nearly knocking over a table laden with coffee mugs as I jumped to my feet.

Other than that, the shoot was a dream, everything I'd ever hoped for. I could have stayed on location forever. But eventually the dreaded final day came round. 'It's a wrap,' shouted Michael, the first assistant. 'Thank you, everybody. Until the next one!'

Schlesinger stepped forward. Casting his eyes about at the chaos of the set, already being dismantled around us, he cleared his throat. 'Wouldn't it be a dream if some time somewhere we could all work together again?' The entire unit started to clap and hoot, and John, nodding, smiling, turned up his jacket collar, shrugged, picked up his script and smoothed the creased pages. Catching my eye he flicked me a small smile, then blew me a whisper of a kiss. I'd learned so much from him; I would forever be grateful for the opportunity he had extended. But now it was time to fold my wings and head home to London. To my little flat, to my ordinary life and to Steve. Other than that I couldn't hazard a guess, didn't have a clue as to what might lie before me.

# Twelve

With the film behind me I had a bit of money, not much, but a start. Enough to send my parents on holiday to Jersey for a week – a modest treat, certainly, but a promise I had made some years before, when they had been very brave words indeed. I'd felt at the time that it would be the least I could do, after putting them through the wringer as I had.

Lady scrabbled at the back of my legs as I breezed around the house, helping to pack.

Mummy watched me, fiddling thoughtfully with her pearl earring, as Daddy hummed to himself, checking out the paperwork for the travel insurance. 'A second honeymoon, Mammy!' he called.

Mummy shrugged. 'Honeymoon?' She reminded him that they had married almost penniless; their wedding breakfast had been two cups of tea and ham rolls. We, my siblings and I, had heard many times about the misery caused by the great depression, the rumblings of war close on its heels. How Mummy had pushed my sister in her pram from Maida Vale to Piccadilly for a job interview, only to find the position had already been filled. She had walked all the way home heavy hearted, only to find Daddy smiling that smile of his. He had flicked her half a crown. 'Where did you get it?' Mummy had asked, but all that really mattered was that it paid for supper, such as it was: two ham rolls and two cups of tea.

'We backed a winner with this one,' Daddy said now, nodding at me. He snapped his fingers, laughing. 'Time to cash in our chips!'

But Mummy was flustered, fussing. 'But how can we leave the dog, the birds?'

Daddy, that kind, sweet man, optimistic as ever, reassured her. 'Johnnie will hold the fort.'

The birds twilling and twittering; the telly on – *Dixon of Dock Green*; Lady looking sheepish in her basket, knowing the all pervading fart was hers; Daddy coughing as he lit yet another cigarette; Mummy and I laughing because as much as I struggled I couldn't quite squeeze into my jeans. Our busy little universe. My sweet old family life. I feel like I am there again.

'So, little one, some rather good news has just come in for you!' said Kenneth a few days later. 'You have to be in LA in thirty six hours.'

He hitched up his trousers over his bulging stomach. His clipped grey moustache seemed to bristle. 'Fox want to test you. The script will be with you this afternoon. It was Stuart Lyons suggested you. Seems he's a fan! You'll be travelling together. He's a decent enough cove. First class tickets, too. I told the casting department, Josephine doesn't know where the back of the plane is!' He leant back in his large leather chair, his hearing aid whistling faintly.

Since his taking me on, I'd had a few meetings with Kenneth. I always felt tense in his presence, although he had never actually made a move. Sometimes, though, he would say things that made me want to pee into his coffee mug, things like 'Does your boyfriend make you come?' or 'What you need is an older man'. But he was a canny, astute agent, and it was considered a blessing to be under his umbrella. So I gritted my teeth and tolerated him the best I could.

'They've booked you into the Beverley Wilshire, he continued. 'Quite the little star, aren't we! Of course, the pay is derisory, but that's the arts for you!' All this with a touch of sarcasm, as if he couldn't quite believe that it was actually me, the client he always addressed as 'little one', who was caught up in all this excitement. I too, momentarily, couldn't believe my ears. This is madness, I thought, jaw dropping... Hollywood! Well, at that moment if you'd tried to put a whole sugared jam doughnut into my open mouth, you would have succeeded easily.

At dawn, a limousine arrived outside my flat. Stuart was already aboard and off we sped together to Heathrow. There was no waiting around on arrival; we were discreetly led to what Stuart told me was the VIP lounge. What luxury, replete with comfortable chairs, a fully stocked bar and complementary cakes! I was tempted, but I knew the girls in Los Angeles would all be skin and bones; I settled for a camomile tea, pronouncing a reluctant 'No thank you' to the proffered iced croissant.

It was first class all the way to LA. Settling into my seat onboard the plane, I couldn't help but marvel, 'It's all so... plush!'

'Thank your agent,' Stuart grumbled. 'Tough bastard. When he pisses, he pisses iced water. Do you know why God made snakes before agents? Because he needed practice!'

Champagne was served after takeoff, and as we reached cruising height, Stuart explained to me the rules of the game. 'You know nothing of Hollywood. Yes, yes, it's as glitzy and glam as you've always imagined, but it's a shark tank. You're there to do a job, so keep your wonder under wraps. The first rule of Hollywood is that movie stars have short careers. And I mean *short*. Don't make the mistake this one actress made. I bought her out myself, she was Canadian, Australian, Antipod... something. Anyway, I had her flown out, I took her to the set for the test, and then what does Miss Antipode do? Go up the star – and when I say *star!* – and she asks him, "Aren't you a bit small to be my leading man?" Stupid cunt. It was back to Botany Bay with that one, let me tell you.'

Emptying his glass and signalling for a refill, he continued, 'Also, before I forget, the young driver who will be meeting us in LA, he's the studio "sneak". Some poof from the mail room who dreams of being head of MGM one day. So silence in the car. You'll be jet lagged, you'll probably be one over the eight. But keep it zipped.' Then he closed his book, off came his glasses, and one Mandrax later he was asleep for the remainder of the journey. But though he was dead to the world, one eye remained open the whole flight, and whatever it was he was dreaming of, it gave him an erection.

Meanwhile I took the script from my bag, sat tight in my seat and set to work. The film was a Western set in Cheyenne, Wyoming. My part was of an English woman, the daughter of the madam of the local brothel. An unpleasant woman, seriously flawed – a great part to play and a real challenge. There would be no sleep for me. 'Please, God, let me not blow it,' I murmured to myself, as far below us the Atlantic Ocean churned. I accepted another glass of champagne and kept on reading.

The next morning, when I hurried down to the hotel lobby, Stuart was already waiting for me. 'How's your jet lag?' he asked, ambling towards me.

'I took a Valium,' I said, raising a finger. 'Just the one. I crashed out at ten then was wide awake at four!'

'Good to go?' he asked, taking my arm and leading me out of the hotel towards the waiting limo, reminding me to watch my words in front of the driver. He didn't have to worry. I was silent the whole way, gazing in amazement out the window at the city. I was in America, the promised land!

We were dropped off at the offices of one of the film's many producers. He was extremely courteous, with a big smile of toilet-bowl-white teeth. 'Pull up your chairs,' he said. 'Let's be friends, get to know each other. Marta, bring some English tea for our beautiful new friend. She's come all the way from London, England.' He beamed at me, revealing every one of his dazzling teeth. 'The land of William Shakespeare!'

To him belonged the honours of conversation, such as it was. His adored children, his soccer team, his charity work, his ailments (oh, spare me), his bitch first and second wives, his alimony horrors... Did he ever run out of talk? But eventually, checking his watch, we moved onto business. 'You will be shooting your test tomorrow, so we need you to meet Kirk.'

'Of course!' I managed, matching his smile.

Kirk Douglas. Spartacus! Aye yai yai!

As the great man was ushered into the office, I could barely believe it was really him.

'Mr Douglas,' I whispered, too breathless to say any more.

'Kirk, please,' he breezed, extending a huge hand.

'Josephine Cagney.'

'Anything to do with Jimmy?'

'Only admiration.'

'He's the best.'

We sank onto a sofa, sitting almost knee to knee. My questions flowed, but he didn't waver once. My character in relationship to the story line, his character in relationship to mine, the history of the period... He was impressed that I had studied the American Civil war as a part of one of my O levels, and taking a shine to me, he offered me some advice:

'I might be Kirk Douglas now,' he said, 'but I was born Issur Danielovitch, a name a little long for above the marquee! You'll meet a lot of people in this industry who'll tell you who you are. What to do, how to be. Don't let 'em!' He wagged a finger in my face. 'If you get this part, Josephine, and I'm sure you will, don't sign for seven. The contract is all on their side. Don't do it! You'll get the part anyway, and once we're done, you'll go home with some moments in your pocket, and totally free of those bastards in their suits.' His eyes twinkled. 'See you on set.'

Who was I to argue with Kirk Douglas? Yes, I did get the part, and no, I didn't sign the contract.

# Thirteen

Kirk was the consummate professional, but at the same time great fun, with a wicked sense of humour. Towards the last week of the shoot, we were in his trailer rehearsing a scene, when out of nowhere he gazed at me with his trademark intensity.

'Josephine, do we fuck?' he asked.

Who was this 'we' he was referring to – our characters? 'I don't know,' I stalled.

'Yes, you do,' he declared, eyes twinkling.

But like all good things, soon the shoot came to an end, and it was back to Blighty for me.

My first day back I went to see Kenneth in his large airy office, with its moulded ceilings, long windows, antique furniture – all elegance, like the man himself. I sat across from him, checking my nails, painted a glossy dark red, waiting for him to finish his calls. I knew what I wanted to say, and when he finally hung up the phone, I was ready.

'I need to talk to you,' I said.

'I need to talk to *you*,' he fired congenially back, proffering two scripts.

I didn't reach out to take them. 'I'm going away for a while, on holiday to the mountains,' I said. His eyes darkened. I persevered. 'Please don't be pissed off with me. I don't want to read another script… I don't want to be tempted.'

All of his geniality had evaporated. He got to his feet and stood over me. He seemed to be calculating, weighing up how to react.

Eventually he spoke. 'Do I understand you correctly? You don't want to work for, what was it, "a while". ' He raised his eyebrows fractionally.

'Steve's film is shooting some scenes in the Dolomites.' I explained. 'He wants me with him, just for the couple of weeks while Carol is in California having new treatment.'

He snorted. 'I wonder why he isn't writing in a part for you?' He laughed derisively. 'You could sort out how much you'd be paid in bed! I am incredibly disappointed in you, Josephine. You've a nasty dose of cock fever. I've seen it all before – talent throwing away its chances. You realise you're only his bit on the side? That you're wasting your precious talent? And more importantly, my precious time?' He dropped his voice, and the angry glow in his eyes waxed a shade brighter. 'I am only trying to help you, Josephine. Steve Weisman, there are three strikes against him. He's Jewish, he's a director, and he's married. A famous player… A cocksman. Who hasn't he fucked?'

I opened my mouth to interject, but he ploughed on.

'Grace Kelly, Deborah Kerr… Do you want the list? This time next year, he won't know your name.' A brief moment of reprieve, then: 'Josephine, you're talented, you're street wise, but you're a pin head minus intelligence.' His tone now was more sad than rancorous, and as he waved his hand, dismissing me from his office, he couldn't meet my eyes.

Turning all the colours of the British flag, I left the office. I didn't turn around to say my piece; neither did I slam the door.

Out on the street, however, I lost my cool. Oh, Christ, the best agent in town, and now I'm on his shit list. I need him… But then, just as suddenly, my heart seemed to swell and harden. Isn't that just how it goes? Isn't that how love appears to the loveless? Like a waste of time, an inconvenience. But I knew different. Mine and Steve's was a love so deep that it felt like our hearts beat as one. 'Bit on the side?' What would he know? Oh, let them smirk. It doesn't matter. Let them sneer. Fuck 'em, that's what I say. I owed him diddly squat.

It was late morning, just before lunch. Music blaring from my radio, I was in the bedroom, packing carefully for my big trip to the Italian Alps. I wanted to look my best for Steve. Silky, tissue-thin underwear, stockings, tiny lace thongs, suspender belts, the red stiletto shoes he loved, the high strappy black patents… I teased myself that I was his bride, and that this was to be our pretend honeymoon! I was just sitting on my suitcase, willing it to close when the shrill ring of the phone made me start up.

'Hello,' I said into the receiver.

'Josephine, it's Dad, he's in the hospital, you'd better hurry.'

Johnny's voice was tight with intensity, broken and low.

'What are you saying? What are you telling me?'

'You'd better hurry,' he repeated haltingly.

'What's happened? Is Mummy with him?' I faltered. 'Please, tell Daddy I'm coming!' I threw on my coat, grabbed my bag and ran down the stairs two at a time. No, God, no, no, no. Please, God, don't let this be happening. I promise, God, I'll be good. Please God...

Frenziedly, I flagged down a taxi 'University College hospital! Hurry! Please!' I didn't say another word the whole way; I just cried like a baby.

My prayers went unanswered. Mummy was waiting for me with Johnny just outside the hospital chaplain's room. I knew before she said a word, by the tilt of her head, the limpness of her shoulders, like a flag at half mast, that I was too late.

'Oh,' she said softly, 'I'll never hear his lovely voice again. I'm so sorry, darling.'

She was shivering with shock. I threw my arms around her, burying my face in her neck. Her voice broken, she whispered, 'He loved you,' and my eyes filled with tears.

'I'm here now, Mummy,' I breathed, my voice deep with sorrow, drawing her close.

'Ellen...' she stammered, 'We must tell Ellen.' My sister had married an American serviceman. When it had come time for them to move to Washington State with their two baby girls, Daddy hadn't been able to bring himself to say goodbye. Instead, he closed himself in his bedroom for three days.

Whispering, Johnny reassured her that a telegram would be sent. I looked at him. Johnny, my little brother, all six foot of him, strong shouldered, his boyish looks now gone, quietly sobbing.

'It was his heart,' he told me. 'He died in his sleep. He didn't suffer.'

Tomorrow, oh tomorrow. And all the tomorrows to follow with no Daddy. How do we live on without the ones we love?

We were plunged into a long day of confusion. Ellen to reach, friends and relatives to tell, questions to be answered, arrangements to make, tears to dry. Around midnight, and with huge difficulty, I managed to get through to Steve. I got him on the phone in his hotel room, exhausted, having just returned from a long day's shoot out on a frozen lake, and after two hours of head to head conflict with his producer. I was falling apart, exhausted, and my memories of what I managed to say are scattered, like those that follow a quarrel. Hunched up like a pitiful orphan, I poured my heart out.

'I'm so sorry, darling, so sorry,' he kept repeating, over and over again in his softest voice. I wanted to fall into his arms. Mummy and Johnny needed me. I had to be the strong one. But I needed Steve. And he wasn't there.

# Fourteen

**M**y little mother broke apart like a dropped piece of porcelain. She was a shadow in a corner, the pain ever present in her sad, dark eyes. My brother, in an attempt to escape reality, fled to America immediately after the funeral. I prayed that my family would heal. As for me, I had to try and get some work, or else I feared this grieving would bring me to my knees.

I had written to Kenneth explaining my situation. I was prepared to eat humble pie, to toe the line and play nice. When I returned to his office again, he saw the change for himself. There were no lights in my eyes; all my usual vivacity had drained away. In silence I looked at my lap and fiddled with the small opal ring on my pinky finger. Even sitting, Kenneth was tall, intimidating. Despite my obvious distress, he showed no enthusiasm whatsoever for representing me again. Oh, how he went on, tossing the points of my letter back to me. His nose twitched and his chins wobbled, and he waffled on about the great and the good he had represented, the innumerable household names covered in lights and glory. About how he remained unimpressed by me, doubted that I had what it takes. His words fell so easily he couldn't have realised their weight. The atmosphere was so icy I could have hacked off a nice little piece to take home with me for my evening cocktail. But then his tone completely changed.

'Okay, little one,' he said, 'welcome back into my stable. Second chance time. I must be losing my marbles. Either that or I'm besotted with you. A touch of both perhaps.'

I laughed uneasily.

He continued: 'And it seems that Granada Television is besotted with you too!' He threw a script across the table at me.

I was so startled I didn't know how to react. 'I don't believe it,' I managed eventually. I flicked quickly through the pages. My heart quickened and my eyes stung, shining as they welled up. I readily turned on my biggest smile and squeaked my thanks. Wearily, and with difficulty, he pulled himself up from his chair, and I rose too. Standing on my tip toes, I kissed him quickly on the cheek. His fingers tangled with mine. 'I think of you as a humming bird,' he whispered into my ear. 'I love you really.'

An immeasurable pause. 'Maybe I know,' I said, trying to mask my embarrassment.

I saw Kenneth again two days later, to accept the offer. He greeted me in ringing tones. 'Little one, today you find me in a mood of forgiveness.' He was so gleeful I was almost worried he might start bouncing around the room. 'I've just signed Rex Harrison!' he announced. 'His previous agent committed the unpardonable error of going on holiday!'

'Why should that be unpardonable?' I ventured pointedly.

'Because I am like a vulture,' he blustered, raising a finger. 'I swooped in, and now he's mine!'

Such hammy acting – I couldn't help giggling.

'As for you, tiny-tits,' he continued, turning his full attention to me. 'If I say terrible things about you, it's only because I love you.'

I squirmed.

'I thought you might be a cuckoo in the nest, the big bird that drives the other chicks to William Morris! But you're back, little one.'

I seized my moment and broke in. 'Who's directing the script?'

'Ted Kotcheff. He's asked particularly for your availability.' Then he was back to his withering sarcasm. 'You're not fucking him as well, are you? You definitely have a type. Viennese Jew, that one.' He snorted.

I ignored this, signed the contract he offered, and bade a hasty exit.

At the funeral, as Daddy's coffin was lowered, Mummy had turned to me and said, 'Live well in Daddy's memory.'

Tearfully, I had replied, 'And for you, Mummy.'

'Yes,' she had said. 'And for me. Oh, Josephine. I must have known what I was doing when I had you.'

# Fifteen

Strange where our passions carry us. Often I have occasion to remember a conversation I had with Iris Fleming, many years ago now. We were having supper in her home. I think I'd been talking about the struggle of auditions. She'd smiled over the top of her glass of wine. 'Darling,' she'd said, her voice mild. 'It is the very struggles of life that define who we are.' A bit trite, I thought at the time, but today they are words I think of often. 'Don't be in such a rush with life,' she'd continued, with an optimistic smile. 'When the time is right, it will happen for you.'

I'm still not sure. Perhaps the paths of our lives are destined; perhaps life's a crap shoot. Back then, I didn't really have time for such arguments. Wasn't I working? And good work too. Three weeks of rehearsal before me, a great script by award winning Liverpudlian Alun Owen, a top-flight director in the Canadian Ted Kotcheff, and fellow actors I could previously only have dreamed of working among: Colin Blakely, Frank Finley, Ronnie Lacy, Alfie Lynch, Billie Whitelaw...

Before the shoot began, Ted had warned me, 'This is your Waterloo.' And I was being challenged alright. As we all relaxed in the bar after a hard day's shooting, I felt Colin's hot breath in my ear. 'I'd better not work with you again,' came his sweet Irish whisper. 'Is it alright if I'm a little bit in love with you?'

'Hmm,' I said. 'Only a little bit? That's okay, I guess, as long as your wife won't mind.'

He replied with a kiss on my cheek.

As I drove home that evening, I oh so didn't want to be going back to my lonely apartment, with no lights on, no Steve waiting for me. On my car radio, Ray Charles was singing 'I Cant Stop Loving You', which wasn't helping my mood. As I crossed Albert Bridge, I thought my dark thoughts. Well, that's how it goes. He isn't mine to love, he isn't mine to love... Perhaps I should have had it printed on a t-shirt. I glanced at my reflection in the rear view mirror. If your lover is a married man, never wear mascara.

It was living a double life. I hadn't dare talk to my mother about Steve. Married man, wife suffering with MS... Any appeal for approval would have been met with just the opposite. Even Victor still shook his head. One afternoon, as we sat at our usual table in Pechon, after listening to me pour my heart out, he lost patience. 'Are you crazy?'

'Only crazy about him,' I replied. 'He says I'm the name on his heart.'

He sighed. 'Are you sure that's not the name of a kiddies' pop song?'

In the thickening silence, he shifted in his seat, studying his brown Chelsea boots. 'Honest to God, darling,' he said eventually, 'I worry about you. He's married. He has a very sick wife. What are you thinking? Where's your sense of decency? More to the point, where's his?'

I flinched, as if I'd been stabbed with a needle. I knew. Let me tell you, I knew. At night there were little voices in my head, tapping away, nasty little throbs of guilt, *tap tap tap*. I would lie there still and silent, accepting my discomfort. I had to try and swallow the bitter along with the sweet. But oh, Steve, call me, Steve, call me.

Quiet and alone, curled up on the sofa, nursing my morning coffee. I heard the rattle of the letter box. Uncoiling myself, I hurried to the front door. Airmail from Steve. When he was away on location, letters were our only connection. Every nerve tingling, I returned to my room and tore open the letter.

'Darling girl of mine,' it read. 'Miss you... Miss you. Hotel fine. Phone impossible. Don't even try! They are treating me like a prince. So far no sweet princess. Please come. Joseph at the London office has the tickets, even the lira or whatever they are. Today's shoot was exhilarating. A mountain I dreamt about in my younger days, well today I looked down on the land from its peak. I climbed the beauty! I'm not that old yet, darling, although sometimes to you I must seem ancient! I'm surrounded by people all day. The crew are an outstanding group but I'm lonely without you. Come share my suite? Can you hear me, Josephine? I need you with me. Carpe diem, my darling!'

Oh yes please! You betcha! I read and reread his letter, before folding it up and placing it in a box high up on a shelf in my cupboard. This was where I kept all of Steve's letters. Sometimes I would take one down and kiss it. Or I'd put it beneath my pillow, and with one hand resting on it, I would finally fall asleep.

Yesterday? Oh, yesterday was *yesterday!* Today I was as bright as a button. I was off to Rome! To Steve!

With a spring in my step and butterflies in my stomach, I checked into the Hotel Inglaterra. It was an old hotel, so quiet, with thick stone walls, gleaming silver bowls of flowers, crisp white linen sheets, and banks of large fluffy white pillows. Most importantly, it was discreet, tucked away from the tourist centres.

'We can't stay at the Excelsior, my first choice. Too many spies,' Steve explained to me that evening, as we ate a room service dinner and shared a bottle of champagne.

'Darling,' I reassured him, 'it's perfectly lovely here. Anywhere, as long as we're together.'

That night, cradled in his arms, I felt a sublime peace. Our lovemaking left me dazed, crying out into the Italian evening. In his dove-soft voice, he whispered, 'If I never have sex again, at least I know what it's like. I'll remember this always.'

He was in the city for three days, meeting with Erio Morricone to decide on the music for his movie. The next morning, he handed me a small mountain of lira for shopping. Oh dear, I thought, tart time. But lira being lira, a huge pile of notes didn't really amount to as much as I thought. On this, our first and only full day together, I was bubbling with excitement, dazzled by the tempo of this ancient city, as police blew their whistles, cars honked, bikes revved, voices were raised and sunlight shone over everything: the bustling coffee shops, the eager fellow tourists, the shop workers clanking up the stutters to their stores. Steve whispered, 'I love you,' as we threw coins into the Trevi fountain. I didn't dare tell him my wish. And he took me to his favourite shop, Battirstoni, where I bought him a tie and two fancy silk handkerchiefs. He then hurried me along to Cerrutti, on the Via Condotti, insisting on a beautiful blue silk dress and jacket. 'The colour of your Irish eyes,' he said. Then on to Feragamo for shoes and the smallest beige crocodile bag. So *expensive...* When I saw the labels, I thought my eyes would pop out.

'Isn't it silly to spend so much?' I asked.

'Of course not, I'm over fifty!' he said, with a faraway smile.

'What's that got to do with it?'

'And I'm closer to sixty than fifty, Josephine. I'm in the danger zone. Let me live while I'm alive.'

His answer threw me. What 'zone' was he talking about? The heart attack zone?

Sometimes these flippant one liners would conceal a note of truth. But for that day I decided to dwell only on the positive. The packages were boxed up, 'Grazie, Grazie Señor, Señora,' was said, and away we flew. Steve flourished his American express card everywhere we went. 'I'm in Rome, my favourite city, with my favourite girl. My one and only.' Like me, he really and truly looked happy, bright and alive. If this was but a dream, please, God, never let me wake up.

All day we stuck to each other, as postage stamps to a postcard too precious to send. Thinking back, from the vantage of the future, we appear to me now as just another couple of fortune's fools, flies on the tail of a run-away horse whose flight we deluded ourselves we could influence.

Rome, a city like no other, dressed in all its colours. We'd spent our days together, and now, for the moment, time was being called. I fingered the small Cartier watch Steve had given me the night before. He'd had a message inscribed on the back: 'I'm with you'. I looked around the beautiful hotel room, all stillness now, quiet in the shimmering morning light. The bed clothes were strewn willy-nilly, the pillows crumpled, a bottle of wine sat half finished on the floor. 'Arrivederci, lovely room,' I said forlornly.

The skinny young porter stared at the scene open mouthed but said nothing. I gave him back the key, along with the few liras I had left, and before leaving, I paused to check the door number. Twenty-seven. From now on, I decided, it would be our lucky number.

The day outside was hot and yellow. As I was driven to Leonardo Da Vinci airport, the eternal city passed by the window, relaxed, carefree, quite unaware that I was clinging to my handkerchief, my eyes blurred by tears, as my heart ached as never before.

It was night time, and I was sitting in the airport lounge, waiting for my delayed flight. I stared out of the window, surveying the horizon. So many goodbyes, so many tears. When you've found what you've always wanted, that's not where the beginning begins, that's where the end starts. I wish I could tell you that I didn't love him. How much I needed to be able say it. To wipe it out, wish him away... But I could never finish the sentence, not even in my own head.

# Sixteen

London. Back to reality.

I left Kenneth's office with a spring in my step. I'd been offered a television play. A two hander written by Alan Plater. I was to play the pregnant wife of young up-and-comer called Michael Caine. Kenneth assured me he was going to be big, having just finished shooting a major movie called *Zulu*. 'Flint sharp ambition,' he warned me. 'You'll have to be on your toes.'

I found Michael to be chatty, with a quick sense of humour, though ultimately he saved his energies for the work. Our scenes were demanding, with neither of us taking any prisoners. Acting with him I had to be as quick as a whip.

After recording, we'd often travel home together, sitting on the top deck of the bus.

'How much are you getting for this?' he asked me one evening.

'Twelve guineas.'

'I'm getting fifteen, so you can put your purse away, this one's on me.'

His gorgeous girlfriend at the time, an actress by the name of Edina Ronay, came to watch the recordings. She could have been Bardot's little sister. In the bar after a shoot, her eyes wide, she'd charm everyone. Michael seemed besotted. He'd sidle up to me, and say, sotto voce, 'Josephine, we're going to shoot off. I want to take Ed for a bite.' We'd hug and tell each other how fabulous we both were. 'Get your bleedin' life sorted,' he'd say, wagging a finger. I'd watch him leave, his arm around her waist, and feel bittersweet. My bloke was in California with Carol. There had been a sudden deterioration in her condition. Taking one last look around the bar, I'd blow a few kisses and steal away.

It was a warm summer afternoon, the first week of September. I was sitting on a train, first class compartment, heading to Brighton to see my actress friend Angela Scoular. We'd met at an audition. She had the most dazzling smile and a wicked sense of fun, and I was looking forward to a larky day.

I leant my head against the carriage window, watching London breeze past. Ramshackle gardens with billowing lines of washing, big red-brick Victorian schools, street after street of identical houses. I tried to catch a brief glimpse of the lives going on behind the windows. A sweet, restful hour stretched ahead of me.

Then in came a man wearing a striped tie in the colours of a salmon and cucumber sandwich. He sat opposite me and we exchanged weak smiles. My first impression of him was that he was very clean, and striking in a compact Anglo Saxon way. Dressed for London, in dark blue linen, with highly polished brown shoes. Lean, middle-aged, older than me by at least twenty years, with sandy hair, a face like a bird, and his eyes obscured by tortoiseshell glasses.

The silence stretched out, filling the space between us. I felt his eyes on me as I gazed out the window. Then he leaned forward and smiled at me.

'May I ask,' he enunciated, his voice rich and melodious, 'do you follow the horses?'

'My father does... did,' I replied.

'Would you put me out of my state of confusion and pick a horse for me?'

He produced a newspaper and, turning it to the racing page, showed me a list of riders and runners. 'Is there a name that jumps out at you?' he asked.

I quickly scanned the list. 'Anything for Eunice,' I said, explaining that Eunice was my favourite aunt's name.

'Good enough for me,' he said with a chuckle. 'I study too much form, sometimes I need to be less well informed.' He waved the paper in the air. 'Well, more haphazard anyway. I believe you are going to be lucky for me!'

He introduced himself as Michael, and we chatted for the rest of the journey. He was extremely courteous, humorous, and he never stopped talking, expressing himself in an almost forgotten idiom. His background was obviously far removed from mine. He quizzed me about my life, and I threw in some theatrical gossip, which seemed to greatly amuse him.

With a screech of brakes, the train announced its arrival in Brighton. The doors opened and suddenly all around us was chaos, with jostling passengers, a squawking posse of children, and waves of chatter appearing as if out of nowhere.

Michael lifted my overnight bag down from the rack above. Taking it off him, I offered my thanks, and with a rather theatrical flourish, he whipped out a business card. 'May I give you this? I shall be awaiting your call.' He was very proper. I accepted it with further thanks. The door opened to the fresh Sussex air, and waving goodbye, he disappeared into the hubbub, still clutching his copy of *The Racing Post*.

I raced to Angela's to tell all. I showed her the small white card; under an embossed crest were the words 'Devonshire of Grieff. House of Lords. Ex. 2590'. Angela yelped with glee. 'An Earl!' she squealed, lighting a cigarette. 'Well, fuck me, an *Earl!*'

'Sit down,' Kenneth instructed before I was hardly through the door. 'Talk to me. What the fuck have you been up to now?'

In my confusion, all I could do was stare mutely.

'I've had his Lordship on the phone,' Kenneth continued. 'Asking me would you be kind enough to call him.' He leant forward. 'I'm your *agent*, Josephine' he said grandly. 'Not a fucking messaging service.' His mouth was fixed in a terrible snarl. 'He says he has something to give you. Oh, I'm sure he does. Perhaps his half-limp aristocratic prick? Makes a change from the circumcised Jew boy, at least.'

I wasn't in the mood for this. I swallowed my first response, but when I spoke my voice was still combative. 'He seemed a very nice man! He gave me his number, I didn't give him mine.'

I took exception the way Kenneth invaded my privacy like this, I really did. Why did I take this vitriol from him? Best agent in town, I kept reminding myself. Though if he thought so little of me, why did he send me yellow roses on St Valentine's Day?

Secretly I was rather flattered that Michael has gone to the trouble to trace me.

'It's like *Brief Encounter!*' Kenneth laughed, slapping his desk 'Well, we bloody well have to hope it is brief!'

Hot water bottle filled, pyjamas on, lights off, I'd just settled into bed when the phone rang. I let it go to my answerphone. It was Michael. 'Hello, Josephine? Good God, it's easier to get through to the Pope!' In his plummy tones he asked whether I would be free for lunch the day after. Would I like to meet him at Wiltons? Say at 12.45? He hoped that I would say yes. The line went dead.

Wiltons? I pictured a stuffy place of dark wood and heavy curtains, the type of place where ancient men went because their fathers had.

The next day I dressed carefully, trying on first one jacket, then another. I went light on my makeup, and was just about to head out the door when I was struck by a pang of guilt. It was only a bit of fun, I reasoned, there was no reason to be secretive about it. I decided to write a letter to my sweet Steve.

'Darling Handsome,' it read. 'It seems so long, sooo long since we were last together. This is a quickie as I'm off to lunch at Wiltons in Jermyn Street. With a man I met on a train! Well, a girl has to eat! I'm such a tart! An Englishman with a capital E! The type you'd dislike on sight. I bet he wears long socks and suspenders. Get the picture? But there's something there... If you don't come back to Blighty soon there might be something more! Just teasing. Though didn't Grace Kelly say that you're incapable of jealously? Even princesses can be wrong, I suppose!'

I re-read it and decided something was missing. I added a funny smiley face underneath my customary heart, and went searching for a spare envelope.

Michael was waiting for me, wearing the same pink and green tie as he had been on the train. Beaming, he handed me a bunch of flowers.

'Oh, you shouldn't have,' I protested.

'It was the least I could do. I'll forever call you Lucky!' He kissed my hand, pulling my chair out for me. Old world manners – was he playing a part?

'Why lucky?' I asked, my face flushing a little.

'Your horse won!'

'It didn't? Blimey O'Reilly!'

Before I knew it, he'd pressed a crisp fifty pound note into my hands. I clapped my hands in girlish delight. I'd never seen a fifty before, and my father would have been more than proud that I'd picked a winner.

We were instantly surrounded by a... What is the collective noun for waiters? Let's say a "fuss". Yes, M'lord this. No, M'Lord that. All speaking at once, over acting, affecting unrecognisable accents – what Noel Coward called Stage Foreign.

Michael ordered my food for me. Whatever it was looked small and white and slid around the plate. The wine flowed and flowed. Then he reached over and closed his fingers over mine.

'Let's clink glasses' he suggested. 'To us.' I didn't know what to say. There was no 'us'.

'To *friendship*,' I said pointedly.

Embarrassed, I picked at my napkin and twiddled my glass.

65

He let out a short breath, raised an eyebrow and looked for a moment as if he were weighing something up. Both elbows on the table, he put his fingers to his temples, and when he spoke again his voice was low.

'There's something I want you to know.' He sat back in his chair. 'I'm a widower. My wife died.'

'Oh, Michael, I'm so sorry.' I reached over the table for his hand and squeezed it. 'When? How?'

'Six years ago. She didn't just die. It wasn't cancer or the suchlike. She... My poor darling killed herself.'

I was stunned that he'd stated it so baldly. He was clearly in the mood to share. He elaborated in his cultured tones every detail I'd have preferred not to hear. I had another glass of wine and listened with a grave face. He told me her name was Salina. They had known each other since they were at Hill House primary school in Chelsea. Each other's first love, they had married in their very early twenties. A perfect match: his father had been at Eton with her father. It was the union of two grand old families. But at love they were beginners, hardly more than children themselves. Not long after their marriage, a daughter, Amelia, arrived. The boy, the girl, husband and wife, now father and mother.

Michael poured out the last of the wine between us and waggled the bottle at the fuss of waiters.

They had been dreamers, he said, always talking about the places they were going to visit, the freedom they would seize before the responsibilities of their estates became theirs. But Salina, it turned out, was a manic depressive. In his lifelong adoration of her, Michael had never seen the signs. From his perspective, her decline was sudden but precipitous, triggered by the birth of Amelia.

Pills, endless pills. Doctors, endless doctors. Days, endless days spent in bed. Living with her had been like riding the rapids. She could appear early in the morning in leather riding boots and a Chanel ball gown, the family jewels on full display, demanding the keys for the car. She could be laughing gaily along with her husband and daughter when suddenly she would shriek, 'You don't know me! My name is Anastasia. I want to be my own person!' and burst from the room.

'Who was the real Salina? The girl I fell in love with, or this hysterical creature? I was never to know. She could be cruel, brutal, callous, or ecstatically happy, wild, loving as could be. In the eighteenth century, she would have been committed to an asylum. But she was the mother of my child, and against all the odds I still loved her.

'It was decided between mine and Salina's parents that Amelia, who by this point was ten years old, was being seriously damaged by her mother's behaviour. She was still wetting her bed, chewing her nails. She'd wake me in the night with her crying. Maybe the answer was to send her to boarding school? Roedean was deemed to be the answer.

'The big day arrived. Amelia's big adventure. The chauffeur, a tall, lean ex-army fellow was waiting with the car. Salina came downstairs wearing her favourite pink robe and matching wedge slippers and put her arms around Amelia, holding on to her without saying anything. I remember she slipped off the yellow ribbon from one of Amelia's plaits, folded it in her hand, and kissed it. Then she opened her arms and moved away. "We won't cry anymore," she said with a sigh. "It doesn't help, does it?" She turned and looked directly at me, eyes glazed with confusion.

' "That's right," I said, "no more tears."

'I kissed her on the cheek, and she looked at me, inscrutable as ever, flashing her half smile. Then without another look for Amelia, she was away inside, back into her impenetrable fugue. And off we went, Amelia to Sussex with only her father and a chauffeur for company.

'The inquest reported that even before my daughter and I had reached the Sussex downs, my wife had dressed, and taken her dogs for their walk down by our lake. They were a mixed bunch, but she always loved them. Tanny, a red setter; Timmy, a poodle; and Tanzy, a mutt. A peculiar thing, before she left she requested lunch to be prepared in time for her return. Poached eggs, always a favourite. And yet she must have had it all planned out already. The police, they told me that the stones she used to weigh herself down, they weren't from the lakeside, they were from the yard.'

After a long silence, punctuated only by Michael noisily blowing his nose, I whispered, 'How did you cope?'

As he spoke he was trembling like a leaf.

'You're expected to feel remorse when you wife dies, especially in such... circumstances. But after the distress of the post mortem, the funeral – in our private chapel, steeped in history – I felt only relief. Her coffin covered in lilies, sitting on a raised dark blue dais. The choir singing "The Lord is my Shepherd", and all my family chanting along – a motley bunch, dressed to the nines, but some of them barely clinging on to life themselves. The heat of the massed candles. The music of the harpist. Hand on heart,' he whispered, 'relief. An overwhelming sense of relief. Her pain was over. I imagined that right that second she was flying on a soft Persian carpet right up to Heaven, where God would welcome her with a cuddle. "No more tears," she'd say. The big bell rings out. Life goes on. We all have to go on and on and on, don't we?'

He broke off, and in the awkward silence that followed, he returned to his food, sucking on a lamb bone, then chewing it as if it were her bones.

# Seventeen

As I stepped through the door, I heard the telephone ringing. I threw down my keys and scrambled to answer it.

'Is that you, Steve?' I asked.

'I'm here, darling. What's with the "*Steve*"?'

'Sorry.' I took a breath. 'I meant darling.'

'That's better,' he said, chuckling. 'You only call me Steve if something's wrong.'

'Nothing's wrong, silly,' I said, lighting a cigarette and looking across the room at his latest bouquet of flowers.

He wanted to know about my week, my friends, my work – all as though nothing had happened. Well, nothing really had happened, had it? Only a lunch, no harm in that surely. 'You know you can always tell me if anything's troubling you,' he said. 'I want to know. Promise me now. I can be with you in twenty-four hours if you need me.'

I sat there, twisting my hair around my fingers.

'I want to whisk you away!' he announced out of nowhere.

'You *do?*' I said. And when I didn't say any more, when I just kept sitting there twisting my hair into knots, he went on.

The long and the short of it was that he had these friends, an up and coming actor by the name of Roger Moore, and his wife, Luisa. They knew about our relationship and, sympathetic of our need for discretion, had invited us to come and stay with them for a long weekend in their chalet in Gstaad.

'It means we can spend three days together before you start rehearsals.'

I'd landed a part in an Anouilh play called *The Scenario*. A first class production by Duncan Weldon, and directed by Stuart Burge. It was work, good work and I had been thrilled to be offered the role. The leading man was to be Trevor Howard. Who would pass on the chance to work with one of our greatest actors? Not me, certainly. I had originally planned to spend the weeks leading up to rehearsals buried in the script. But the mountains of Switzerland, Steve's arms... I couldn't say no.

I flew out on the earliest plane I could find. Stepping from the taxi outside a cosy-looking chalet, I was greeted warmly by Steve's friends. Luisa was vibrant, typically Italian – quick to anger, but so friendly, welcoming and attentive, her eyes bright with amusement as she looked me over. Roger, meanwhile, was the sweetest of men – a joker, gentle, self-effacing – oh, and of course, one of the world's best lookers. He and Louisa had three lovely children, and as a family they split their time between a variety of luxurious homes all over the world.

Things change, of course. Life for Roger and Luisa, Luisa and Roger would warp: no longer love and laughter, now broken hearts, broken dreams. But that's another story, and it isn't mine to tell.

So, there we were, Steve and I and his glamorous friends, living a touch of the high life. I hardly had time to unpack. That first evening we were off to a party at Valentino's house. That's right, *the* Valentino.

Luisa didn't feel my Gina Fratini dress was 'appropriato'. 'Darli,' she said, 'you look like a peasant.'

She took me into her immense walk-in wardrobe, a double room really, insisting I borrow a silver and black Valentino tuxedo. She backcombed my hair, added more blender to my cheeks, gloss to my lips, picked up the largest bottle of Chanel No5 I'd ever seen and sprayed me top to toe. Allora! Perfecto! Signora Moore felt I was good to go.

The great designer's house was cut high into the side of a mountain. As we approached, the car bore left onto a narrow track. Several men in matching lederhosen and green jackets were waiting to receive us with a torchlight procession. Feeling the chill of the evening breeze, we urged them to hurry up to the house. But they could have dawdled forever and I still wouldn't have been ready for the sight that met when I stepped inside.

This was an Aladdin's cave of splendour, glamour and comfort. Valentino could certainly lay on a swish affair. His little black book must have been bursting with the numbers of the great and good. Here in the main drawing room were a sea of famous faces, celebrities with a capital C. Here they were able to shut out the prying eyes of the world, to let their hair down, be themselves. What on earth was I doing there. It seemed I was the only guest who wasn't a legend.

As if on cue, a soft voice came from behind me. I turned, only to be met by the sight of Audrey Hepburn. She looked weary, and I couldn't help but notice that her hands had loved a garden or two. To my astonishment, she asked me for my autograph.

'Wh-who me,' I stammered. 'You don't want me. I'm just a friend of Roger's.'

'It's for my son,' she said, as if that explained everything.

'Oh, how old is he?'

'He's thirty-one.'

*How quaint,* I thought. Perhaps children of the stars take longer to grow up?

As I perused the buffet, I was startled by the extravagant rings on the fingers of the woman browsing next to me. Looking up, I took a sudden intake of breath, as I realised I was gazing upon the exquisite face of Elizabeth Taylor.

'The most terrible thing happened just this morning,' she informed me.

As it turns out, the most terrible thing was she'd broken one of her fingernails. 'Right off!' she exclaimed, holding up her right forefinger so I could see the band-aid.

I tried my best to look past the sparklers on her fingers, and attempted to appear sympathetic – a real test of my acting prowess. To mask my bemusement, I remarked on how stunning her aquamarine and diamond necklace was.

'Oh, Dennis gave me that,' she replied nonchalantly. 'And while they were wrapping it up, he bought me this!' She raised her wrist to show me a bracelet glittering with iridescent diamonds. She shrilled with delight then accosted one of the serving staff. 'Any more chocolate ice cream?' She was gorgeous, resplendent in all her finery. And of course I was star struck, which I hoped my trembling plate didn't betray.

Dennis, the generous boyfriend, flushed face, grey hair, and a big tummy bulging under his frilly white shirt, was sitting on one of the sofas, his bejewelled companion beside him. A fellow guest approached them. I could barely believe what I heard next.

'Dennis, have you had a good year?' the guest asked cheerily.

Dennis rolled his cigar slowly and deliberately to the other side of his mouth. He patted Elizabeth's knee. 'You ask me if I've had a good year,' he said venomously, 'when I've ended up with *her!*' Well, you couldn't make it up!

Steve was huddled in a corner with Frank Sinatra. They had made a picture together a few years before. Steve beckoned me over and introduced me. Frank rose a little unsteadily to his feet. 'Josephine, it's my pleasure, but keep your distance. I'm afraid I've a terrible cold.' Oh, I felt so cheated. Sneeze on me, Frank, sneeze on me!

Howls of laughter came from a side room, where Peter Ustinov was holding court. An adoring group of guests listened enraptured, hanging on his every utterance. His wife, however, was sitting stone-faced, evidently bored silly, having heard Peter's stories far too many times before.

I passed David Niven on the way to a bathroom. 'Alright, Mummy?' he asked, arching his neck to look back over his shoulder. *He's looking at my bum*, I thought

Charlton Heston's wife, apparently unwell, didn't stir from her chair the whole evening. Charlton was very attentive, never leaving her side, even as everyone began to congregate around Charles Bludhorn of Gulf and Western Oil, who had just bought Paramount Pictures. Everyone wanted to pin him down, impress him – they were like bees swarming around their queen. Not Steve, though. He never did play the sucking up game.

I was sitting on a large velvet chair, on the outside looking in, when Montgomery Clift came over, carrying a glass of champagne for me. He perched on the arm of my chair. 'You look lonely,' he said.

He was tall, marvellously handsome in his neat black dinner suit, and softly spoken, with beautiful manners.

'I feel a bit spare,' I told him, 'out of my depth. I don't know what I'm doing here.'

'We all feel that in situations like this.'

'You too?'

' 'specially me. I don't know what the hell I'm doing here. 'lizabeth insisted. She's like my sister. Better than a sister.'

'What about him,' I asked, nodding over at Dennis.

'Oh, he's just her latest mistake. It won't last. Then I'll dry her tears till the next jerk comes into view.'

'Not much fun for you,' I ventured.

'Fun? We all get our fun in different ways. Me? Acting the best I can, drinking as much as I can. You know, honey, men such as me live under a cloak – 'specially in Hollywood. The agents and the studio put you out with girls. All pretty, mostly dumb. That's how I first met Elizabeth. She was the prettiest girl in all the world... But I think it's time for a drinky pinky.' He took a hip flask from his pocket. 'Can you reach for the orange juice?

'Don't fall for the money or the jewels,' he sighed, sloshing a liberal dose of clear liquor into his glass. Elizabeth will be lonely when she loses that brightness. I'll look after her, of course. If I live. Car crash didn't kill me, but this potato will.' He said this as though he was talking about the weather and took a swig of his drink. I followed his gaze. Elizabeth's bejewelled wrist beckoning.

'On parade, darling,' he said wryly. Standing, he offered me his hand. 'Hope we meet again during your stay.' He made to leave, but hesitated. 'Steve's very talented,' he said. 'I owe him a lot. But he's never going to change. You should know that.'

I nodded, surprised at his seemingly genuine concern.

Then he was gone, across the room to Elizabeth's glittering persona.

Two men walked past me, and I overheard one tell the other, 'Haven't seen Al for a while. His office is closed.'

His companion muttered back, 'Christ, haven't you heard? The poor bastard fell off the Matterhorn.'

I looked for Steve. There he was, still palling around with Sinatra. Someone shouted from across the room, 'Give us a tune, blue eyes!'

Frank held his hand to his throat, pantomimed a delicate cough and shook his head with a smile.

'What's a party without a serenade!' the voice persisted. A cheer went up in the room. Sinatra made an affected groan, stood and walked to the piano. He smoothed his throat with his hand.

'So long as it's in B flat.' He tinkled the keys. Suddenly I felt Steve's arms wrap around me. Sinatra sang 'One for My Baby' and my baby held me. This was happiness. This was Steve's world. Let the party go on… go on… go on.

# Eighteen

Frozen in my memory, with the stillness of a painting. The phone had rung in the darkness just before dawn. It was Kenneth. He spoke quickly, his voice like the buzz of a wasp. 'Little one, you know I love you, I will always love you, I will always look after... Errr... I've just had a call from Wasserman on the coast and... Very early this morning, oh, err... I hate to be the bearer of bad news but, there is no other way, nothing other than to say it... Darling... Steve's dead.'

*Five, ten, fifteen* went the beats of my heart. I could say nothing. I just stood there, as if the floor was sucking me down.

And then the button was released. I screamed, *roared*, 'Say it's not true!' I felt the beginnings of sheer panic, edging toward terror. Through my gasping sobs, I could still hear Kenneth droning:

'The plane he was on... No survivors... Crashed into the High Sierras... Poor visibility. I'm sorry, darling, sorry to be the one to tell you... A great talent, and you loved him, of course... I'm not sure whether you want to go over for the service... My advice... So sorry... But perhaps best to stay away.'

I didn't want to hear this. I stood up so swiftly, I went dizzy. I dropped the phone to the floor and ran towards the bathroom. Clutching the cold rim of the toilet bowl, I threw up.

God in heaven help me, he'd gone.

Life went on around me. So few people in my life even knew about Steve. With sombre faces, Liz sympathised, Victor held my hand. They tried their best. But I knew they had always disapproved of Steve, and that secretly they thought I was better off.

Victor held me, reassuring me that I'd find someone else in time, then after a moment adding, 'Just don't go looking for the same kind of man, that's

74

all.' Meanwhile my heart was in ribbons. He had been my secret love; now all I wanted was for the world to know all about us. What we had been. What we had had.

I hid myself away. I felt I could no longer trust myself in the outside world. I knew that if I ventured outside, at the sight of the first stranger I might scream, I might burst into tears, I might confess everything.

I must have spent nearly a month like that, ignoring the phone, the doorbell, keeping the curtains closed. It seemed to me sometimes that I was moving through a dappled world, where one moment everything was too bright, the next pitch black. But then one morning when the phone rang, and as I just happened to be passing, without thinking I answered it.

It was Victor. 'Don't give me any of your excuses, no ifs or buts, get your knickers on and meet me at Pechon at eleven thirty.'

*Click*, the line went dead.

When I arrived he was wearing a pink linen jacket, navy Bermuda shorts, long navy socks and black loafers, plus his squashed, worn Panama. He looked like an overweight American tourist on holiday. It was the first time I'd wanted to laugh in weeks.

'This can't go on,' he said as I took my seat. 'It's three bloody weeks since I read Steve's obit in *The Times*. Glowing, of course, better than I'll get. But it's time to get back to the party, Josephine.'

I piled up my hair with my hands only to again let it fall again. 'Grief demands an answer,' I said. 'Sometimes there just isn't one.'

But undeterred, on Victor went. I must get my mind back on my work, he kept saying, reminding me of how proud my mother was of me, how I couldn't afford to slip down the rungs of the theatrical ladder. He leant forward and took my hand. Looking into my eyes, he said, 'You know you're going to get over this, so why not start today? I know you're one of these actors who thrive on instinct. You haven't had the disadvantage of proper training. Some of those so called drama teachers think Chekhov is a town in Russia!' He faltered, then rediscovered his thread. 'He was a great man and a great writer. Remember this opening of *The Seagull*? The man says to the woman, "Why do you always wear black?" and the silly woman replies, "I'm in mourning for my life." ' He smiled. 'You're far and away from being a silly woman, Josephine, but you are in danger of becoming fork bendingly boring. Next time I see you, I want you vivacious, in full makeup!'

Self-consciously, I touched my face. I had neglected to put on any makeup. But it was for the best, as again the tears rolled.

The next afternoon, I was wandering down King's Road, when I saw someone waving frantically in my direction. It was Ali, an actress I had worked with a couple of years before. It was a delightful surprise. I'd heard she'd married an American actor, Gary Meadmore, and that they now mostly lived in California. We fell into each other's arms then headed into the Chelsea Potter.

I wasn't exactly crying into my Merlot, but after a couple of glasses, I was in full flow, sharing all my woes. I had the impression that she found my outpourings, my desire to confide, less than utterly enthralling. But as I broke off, she nodded sympathetically, and digging in her pocket, she produced a card.

'Gary and I know someone who can help you,' she said, handing me the card. 'Can we give you a call tomorrow morning?'

I nodded, and after finishing our drinks, we kissed goodbye, and I walked to the Underground.

As promised, early the next morning, my phone rang. 'Josephine,' said a Southern voice down the receiver.

'Yes, that's me.'

'It's Gary, Ali's husband.'

'It's kind of you to call.'

'Not at all. I empathise with you. And I truly believe I can help you through this difficult time.' He paused. 'Did you know that Jesus is alive and living in New York?'

I had to pinch myself to make sure I wasn't dreaming. '*What?*' I said. 'What are you saying?'

'Jesus. I talked to him last night. He's recently got divorced. I told him about you, and he says you should call him.'

I was at a loss for the words. The man was utterly deranged. 'How did you meet him?' I managed eventually.

'A friend of mine met him in Macy's, in the food hall. Jesus told him to sell up and move to LA. He did, and now he never stops working!'

I decided I had indulged him long enough. Chirpily, I said, 'Sounds too good to be true.'

'I know you don't believe me,' Gary persisted, 'but I've got a direct line, person to person. The word with God, Josephine, is that his spirit moves. Jesus tells me with authority. It is not faith, it is fact. You need the Lord and you need him *now!*'

I could almost feel his finger wagging in my face.

'It's not that I don't believe you, Gary,' I placated him. 'It's just that I need a little time to think this through.'

'He reminds me, "Suffer little children and let them come to me!" '

'Forgive me, Gary, but this is over my head.'

'It's not your head he's after. It's your heart!'

I hung up the phone. What a lunatic!

But a couple of months later, something strange happened to me. I had taken myself off to California for a week. Driving towards San Simeon, the legendary home of William Randolph Hearst, I saw a figure moving through the woods, carrying a large wooden cross.

No, I hadn't been drinking. No, I wasn't tripping. But as I stopped the car, my head *was* spinning. Blinking, I looked again into the woods. The figure had disappeared. *I've got to get away from here,* I thought.

Wherever I go, if Jesus wants me, he knows where to find me.

# Nineteen

Memory piles upon memory like layers of rock. Only shards remain visible. I took Victor's advice. I went back to work. Connecting with my characters, with people whose lives were far removed from mine, helped shake me from my numbness.

Kenneth pulled out all the stops, using his connections to keep me in continual work. He'd ring me every few days. 'A role has come up,' he'd say, and that would be the first I'd heard of even being in the running. 'You start next week.'

'Got another one for you,' he announced once day. 'It's the production of these two obnoxious Arab twins. They're naked liars. I wouldn't trust them with William Morris's cock! I'll ask for the money up front. And special billing. "*And* Josephine Cagney". How does that sound? "*With* Josephine Cagney".'

I needn't have been alarmed. The Arabs were courtesy personified, and soon after Kenneth rang to say that they had loved me, and that he had agreed a fabulous deal.

'I assume you're on-board,' he asked. 'After all, it's three weeks in the Caribbean…'

As I stepped off the plane it was raining. Not what I'd been hoping for from Jamaica! I was met by a young man, a child really, a lanky, dark-eyed, freckled American who introduced himself as Joe. He was dazzlingly good looking in his blue-grey cowboy hat. As we dashed for cover from the tropical rain, he informed me he was the third assistant director on the film.

Before tourism had taken over, Ocho Rios had been a fishing village. Now it was to be our base of operations. It was postcard pretty, wrapped around an idyllic, un-spoilt bay. The hotel, however, was all faded colonial grandeur, the glamour long gone. The pathways were overgrown, the floor tiles cracked, the paint peeling and dead insects on the window sills. Despite the Caribbean climate, it still somehow managed to have the chill of a cheap hotel.

Still, I had to make the best of things. And make the best of things I did. For three weeks, I was able, on my many days off, to swim with dolphins, have lunch with Noel Coward at his villa, and be enchanted by the humming birds feeding from the flowers.

The first day of shooting, I was up at five thirty in the morning, and in the makeup trailer not long after. Nicky was my makeup artist. A beautiful curvaceous blonde, she loved nothing more than to prance around in the tightest of hot pants and the smallest, most inadequate of bras. Every day the colours changed: orange with turquoise, violet with red... She certainly knew her job. She always made me look absolutely radiant. She proved to be a friend, a real charmer, and a total nymphomaniac. But hey, we were on location, and what happens on location stays on location.

I'd been cast as the wife of one of the lead characters, who was played by an actor I'm going to call Mace. 'Mace' was American, a good-looking six-footer with green eyes, blue jeans, black cowboy boots, and a small pouch of marijuana always swinging from his belt. He was arrogant, mocking, and always seemed to be pacing around as if his life had become a cage.

I'd had it whispered in my ear that, when he'd heard of my casting, he'd said of me, 'She's too fucking old to be playing my wife.' He was easily eleven years older than me, so as I walked shyly on to the set, I was ready for trouble.

We were to shoot a scene in which I had most of the dialogue. A scene I had looked forward to playing, strong stuff, something I could get my teeth into. But every step, he seemed to go out of his way to undermine my performance. Oh, what games *didn't* he play! He'd stand in my light, fiddle with props mid-scene, question my pronunciation of certain words. When I was having my close-ups, he'd mutter. 'You can't do it, can you? You weren't first choice. You've blown it, blown it for me, blown it for everyone.' He particularly liked to remind me that he had balls, 'big ones' – exactly what I wanted to hear!

I lost my temper just once, turning to our director for support. 'I can play it blue, I can play it green, but who's directing this sodding film?' I snapped.

It made no difference. The director just shrugged, and seeing this, Mitch was only encouraged. He pulled a door from its frame, threw furniture. Did he ever hit me? Not quite, but at one point during a scene, he hooked a finger though the short gold chain round my neck and pulled me sharply towards him. The wine on his breath almost made me puke. Again, I turned to our director for support; again, he turned a blind eye. I was on my own, left dangling. The most I'd ever get was the miming of scissor movements, his way of telling me that Mace's scenes would be cut out. Except, of course, that they were my scenes too. The producer sometimes tried to step in, but there were no teeth to anything he ever had to say; Mace was the star, and boy did he know it.

Mace and I were unhappily yoked together for the duration of the shoot. Unhappily, that is, until five days before the filming was over, when we were called for a night shoot.

Our scenes completed, four of us – Mitch, two other actors and myself – lay back on the grass at the top of a cliff. The sea sparkled in the moonlight below. One small fishing boat swayed along. The sky seemed to be raining stars.

A bottle of wine was passed between us, and Mitch lit the first of several fat joints. Jokes were shared, boasts told, about the work we'd done, people we'd worked with. Our giggles seemed to float on the breeze. It must have been close to dawn, the mist rising off the ocean, when Mitch lumbered to his feet. Standing over me, he announced, 'Come with me.'

Was I stoned? Oh, who cares. Who knows what was going on in my head. Certainly not me. The other two actors sat up on their elbows and watched as Mitch leant down and scooped me up into his arms, carrying me back to the hotel and my room.

Where we stayed for the twenty-four hours.

The night passed in a sexual frenzy. It seemed we would never be satisfied. During the next five days, before we had to fly home, he taught me a new sexual language. And how sweet it was.

As a lover he was the polar opposite to how he was as an actor. He was affectionate, gentle, giving. 'Perfect,' he'd say, staring at my cunt, 'it's just perfect.' He'd begin slowly. Breathing gently, I'd feel as though I was sinking into a cloud. Then he'd flip me over, and my face pressed into the pillow, he'd enter me all the way.

We were drunk on each other. It was like being inside of a wave – a warm, embracing, liquid place all softness and undulation.

Relationship? That's too strong a word for it. It was just a few stolen days. As soon as the shoot was over he was back to London and his model fiancée. Two years later, I was sad to read in the papers that he'd died of a massive heart attack.

When I think of Mace, I think of Caribbean sunlight, so bright it's almost blinding. But a shadow soon falls over the scene. The shadow of Steve.

# Twenty

One stormy evening just after Christmas I had dinner with Michael at The Ritz. He greeted me with his arms open wide. Champagne was ordered, glasses clinked, the menu studied.

'M'Lord, we have grouse this evening,' the young waiter said.

'Marvellous, then its grouse for two,' Michael ordered breezily.

My heart sank. 'Not for me, please,' I said.

'But it's the season,' he insisted.

'No, sorry, Michael, I don't eat little birds. Fish and vegetables for me, please, that would be lovely.'

That evening Michael was particularly congenial, solicitous of how I had been doing. I told him of the beauty of the Caribbean, the charm of Noel Coward, the magic of the hummingbirds. 'Did you know they can fly backwards?' I avoided mentioning Mace. I didn't think Michael would respond very well to hearing I'd just had the best fuck of my life.

In a brief lull, Michael informed me that, apart from being a landowner, he was one of the country's top importers of South African wine.

'It's a nice little earner,' he said. 'And I have some wonderful staff – I barely have to lift a finger. Then suddenly he was serious. 'That reminds me, would you host a private dinner party for me, here at The Ritz?'

I was taken aback. 'I'd be delighted,' I managed. 'But why not ask—'

'I'm asking you,' he replied firmly.

'Who is the party for, what will you be celebrating?'

'I want to treat my top eight sales reps and their wives, as a well done and a thank you.'

'What a generous thought.'

'Ask me who the guest of honour will be,' he coaxed.

'Prince Philip?' was all I could think of to say. 'Don't tease, tell me.'

He leant forward across the table, savouring knowing something I didn't.

'Neil Armstrong,' he boomed, slapping the table.

I thought he was joking. '*The* Neil Armstrong?'

He explained: he liked his dinners to have a certain sparkle. He was paying Neil Armstrong some inordinate sum of money to make an appearance. Cursorily, he started to mention a fee for me, but I quickly headed him off. 'Speak to Kenneth,' I said, 'I don't do money.'

I lit a cigarette as he ordered another glass.

According to him it was to be my event from start to finish.

'Your personal touch is what I'm looking for,' Josephine,' he told me. 'It's the only thing missing.'

'Budget?'

'Whatever it costs, it costs. I want it to be an evening to remember.'

The next morning, at the crack of sparrow fart, I started drawing up to-do lists.

I decided it was to be a black tie evening. A pianist would be needed, and a head chef to help design a menu, and a sommelier... The delightful Kenneth Turner to design the flowers and trees – yes, *real* trees. Climbing jasmine, baskets of lavender, tumbling English roses... The room to be lit by candle light, and invitations and menus to be printed by Smythson. Butler and Wilson for moon themed gifts: earrings and brooches for the women, cuff links for their husbands.

Me? I went to Edina Ronay for the most beautiful red silk dress. Michael lent me diamond earrings and a matching diamond bracelet from his family's coffers. And because of Kenneth's talent for the deal, I was to be paid £1000, not to mention receiving a suite in the hotel for three nights.

I had asked my mother to share the suite with me. Those past few months, whenever I had visited, she had been withdrawn, but when she saw the room her face lit up.

'This is what I call living,' she said with a laugh. She had cried so many tears, to hear her laughter was delicious. Briefly, her delight lent her youth again. I saw my mother, the mother who had loved to dance with my father. I had almost forgotten her.

The party was the night before St Valentine's. All day I was busy-busy, running up and down the back stairs, calling out requests, instructions, questions, corrections. With only minutes to spare, we were ready for the show.

Soft piano music in the background, I surveyed the scene with pride.

Michael, in his best bib and tucker, appeared by my side and put his arm around my waist, beaming his approval as we welcomed the guests. They weren't especially scintillating people, but they all wanted to have a good time. Excited chatter, laughter, glasses clinking... And of course, centre stage, Neil Armstrong himself.

Neil had a gentle, self-effacing presence. Naturally we all hung on his every word. Obligingly he answered every question, expanded on every point, and reeled off anecdote after anecdote. At one point in the evening, I remember he told me, 'You can kill the dreamer, but you cannot kill the dream.' I scribbled it in my notebook at my first opportunity. Before taking his leave, he even signed autographs.

As his hostess, I walked him to the lift. 'It's been amazing to meet you,' we said in unison. Laughing, we embraced for the briefest of moments.

'Josephine, do you always have this effect on men?' he said with a wink.

But just as I was about to answer, 'Not *all!*' The lift doors closed, and my man on the moon was away into nothingness.

The evening was a razzle-dazzle success. I had seen the last of the guests to the door, and hours before said goodnight to my mother. Returning to the function room, I found Michael sprawled in a chair, tieless, with his shirt collar open, and his black velvet jacket hanging unbuttoned. 'Great evening,' he said. 'You did a first class job. I'm proud of you – a very happy man.'

He chuckled, then leant forward, holding out a hand for me to take. 'Let's go to your room for a cuddle,' he suggested in hushed tones.

I recoiled. 'No, Michael, absolutely not. No cuddles, nothing.'

'Oh, come on. A little bit of loving would be the perfect ending to the evening.'

'Was this part of your plan?' I demanded.

He squirmed a little in his chair. 'In a way,' he admitted sheepishly.

'What way exactly?' I insisted. He'd touched a nerve. A door had slammed between us.

'Don't play the little virgin, Josephine,' he suddenly erupted. He'd been drinking all evening, and I felt his anger radiating off him as an arctic chill on my skin. Things might turn nasty.

I tried to placate him, to lighten things up with a joke. 'Anyway,' I said breezily, 'we don't want wake up my mother!'

He was bemused by this, not seeming to grasp the connection. 'What's your bloody Mother got to do with anything?'

'She's been staying with me.'

'Your mother's in your bedroom?' He stared at me in disbelief.

'Yes,' I explained. 'I wanted to get her out of the house, take her mind off things.'

He looked utterly deflated. I seized my moment, leaning forward and kissing him on the forehead, as if he was a child being put to bed. Then I slipped out the room before he could recover. Thank God for my mother! But how could I have been so naïve? Me, who'd been round the course more than once.

When I told Kenneth, he couldn't suppress a shriek of laughter. 'You moved your *mother* in? Big mistake – his Lordship wanted to get his leg over!'

Our three day retreat over, I had bid an affectionate goodbye to my mother and was walking home. The weather was bitter, and as I fought through the elements, I went over and over Michael's actions in my head. I just couldn't understand him. Why had the silly bugger soured such an enjoyable evening. The *arrogance* of his assumption that I would just fall into bed with him! Had I ever led him on to believe that I would fuck him, *ever?*

Fumbling in my pocket for my keys, I hurried up the front steps, only to find, propped up against my door, the most glorious bouquet of tumbling blooms. I tore open the small envelope attached, and read the words written on the white card: 'Please forgive the clumsy pass. I'm out of practice. Can we blame it on the drink? In a blaze of optimism, I've booked a table for dinner at Le Caprice. Tomorrow at 8 o'clock. Please join me? Michael.'

Why did I go? Good manners? I'm not even sure myself. Perhaps I felt sorry for him. In the end, I suppose, it doesn't matter. Life is about the dos and the don'ts, the dids and the didnt's. I went. It's as simple as that.

As I approached the table, Michael beamed at me. 'Oh, it's so good to see you, Josephine!' he said. 'Can we start again?'

But I was on my guard. He had misinterpreted our relationship once. I made sure my assent sounded appropriately grudging. The waiters fluttered around us, almost cooing with solicitousness. Michael, I think, was so pleased I'd turned up that he barely stopped babbling the whole evening. Everything he said had a humorous twist, a thorny wit, and despite myself, I began to be amused by him.

We ended up swapping stories about ourselves. On top of their vineyard holdings, his family also owned a whiskey distillery. 'Comes in handy at Christmas,' he said with a wink.

I told him that, one day, I'd like to try my hand at honest writing.

'Oh, that's a difficult life,' he said. 'Writing is ideal reality, and life is far from ideal.'

I nodded my head, though I had no idea what he was talking about.

'What's it like to be the prettiest girl in the room?'

I considered being demure, playing the lady. But remembering that he had hardly been the perfect gentleman himself, I decided to be honest. 'It's the best,' I said, winking. 'But it's never enough.'

I told him the last play I'd been in was a turkey.

'What's a turkey?' he queried

I chuckled. 'Well, not a bird with feathers!'

He laughed at this, then apropos of nothing, asked, 'Are you C of E?'

'Daddy was Irish, I'm a lapsed Catholic. I haven't been to confession in I don't know how long.'

'We're a devout Catholic family,' he broke in. 'Irish originally, but we never took the soup.'

'You've lost me now,' I said.

He continued, as if to a child. 'When Oliver Cromwell ransacked Ireland he offered a bowl of soup to the starving. If, of course, they would change their faith, become Protestants. My family refused to take the soup. Oh, it's history now, but some things don't change, they go on and on.'

He told me he was sent away at thirteen. 'To Ampleforth,' he said. 'Very prestigious, of course, but it didn't stop the posh prods at Eton sneering at us. They called Ampleforth "Harrow with monks!" ' He shook his head, looking into the middle distance. 'You might not believe this, but I was a pretty boy, blonde, "a crush boy" as we were called. You fagged for the prefect and then became his crush.'

I could barely believe what I was hearing. Why was he telling me this? Perhaps he thought he owed me some kind of explanation for his behaviour the other evening.

'I was his to be used,' he continued. 'It was just the way of things. Tradition. *Tradition* the result of which I had a nervous breakdown – undiagnosed, of course, at the time. Depression.' He drained his glass. 'What Churchill called "the black dog".' A moment's pause while his glass was refilled. 'This I timidly offer not to excuse, but to explain my clumsiness. I have suffered from a lack of... adventure in the bedroom department. I know only what I've been shown by others. And I have not always been shown kindness.'

All his scabs were coming off now. I could think of nothing to say.

The unravelling continued. He chewed his steak, then mumbled, 'Tobias,' naming his adored elder brother. He'd been killed in a car accident in Argentina while off on his gap year. I waited. This thought seemed to have quietened, sobered him.

'Startlingly, I found I was now the heir to, well, everything.' For a moment he seemed ancient. 'For my mother it was a disaster. Her favourite son dead. She made me feel like she wished I'd been the one in that fucking car. She probably did.'

He leant forward, raising his glass. 'To Mother,' he said, draining his glass again. Then, with a refill, 'To Mother.' And again, and again a third time. 'That nightmare woman. I'd have known more love had I been the son of a whore.'

A long silence followed, adding only volume to his next words. 'After Salina died,' he told me, 'for years I went through life looking over my shoulder for her shadow. I could do friendship and fucking, but I simply would never have imagined letting myself care so much that I could be hurt again. No one person could ever be that important. But I wasn't reckoning on you.'

A slow and warm smile began to spread across his face. 'I'm too long in the tooth to be playing games,' he said evenly, 'but I feel like I'm one of those damn silly love songs. Tomorrow and tomorrow and tomorrow... What else is there for me but you? I've made up my mind. If I don't have you, I have nothing.'

I cut him off. 'I just don't feel like that about you,' I said, as delicately as I could.

'I know,' he said. 'But I'll grow on you. I'm pinning my flag to the mast, I'm asking for a chance. That's all.' He gave me a weak smile.

'But what do we have in common?' I protested. 'Apart from both of us having loved and lost?'

'Isn't that enough?' He said sombrely. 'We understand each other's pain. We understand that we are here and they are not. We're in the same boat, Josephine, and we both know that we must be very careful not to tip it over.' He reached around the table, picked up one of my limp hands from my lap, and with a smooth fingertip, he traced the lines of my palm.

'Pretend I'm Prince Monolulu,' he said, with a smile that twitched his slightly crooked nose.

'Who's that?'

'The psychic palm reader.'

'What do you find?' I asked.

In a cackling, witchy voice, he replied, 'It says, Josephine, your goose is cooked!'

Laughing at the hamminess, I reached for my glass. 'Can't say I haven't been warned!'

'Shall we go to the Ritz casino, tumble a few dice, see if you're still lucky for me?' A joyous shine enlivened his sad eyes as he peered up at me from under his mop of fair hair. I'd caught just a glimpse of a fleeting brightness in them, the ghost of his youth.

# Twenty-One

Kenneth was a man who could have a row with an empty room. Whenever I went to see him, it was like flipping a coin: was I to receive a job offer or another lecture? On this particular occasion, it seemed the latter.

'Little one,' he blustered, 'you were seen at Le Caprice with that Duke or whoever the fuck he is, flashing his Amex card.'

'Hello, Mr Snoop!'

He ignored this. 'I want to remind you about that B movie actress, the pretty brunette – you worked with her in LA. What was her name?'

'Pauline something,' I said, not quite following the drift of his thoughts.

'Hers was an earl, I think – Catholic too. She got the sable coat, the Aston Martin, the title, the country estate, five children. Then the poor bitch lost her mind, and she got taken away by the little men in white coats.'

His voice, normally so pompous, was a low, tired drone. For once, he didn't seem to be relishing his lecture. He paused. Then, pointing his gold pen in my direction, he ventured, 'I was just thinking, that's all. The rumour around town—' He leaned in close to me, lowering his voice and affecting concern.

I cut him off. 'What rumour?'

He didn't like being interrupted. Instantly his mood soured. 'That your earl is a hopeless fuck,' he spat. 'Impotent and an alcoholic, is that what you want?'

I held up a hand. 'And who exactly is spreading this rumour?'

He shrugged. 'The usual. Tarts working Shepherd's market, Churchill's...'

'You have their numbers on speed dial, I imagine,' I retorted.

The silence between us was heavy. He'd gone too far this time – gone from ruffling feathers to plucking them. Without another word, I left his office. Out in the street, I stood panting shallowly – not fighting for breath but struggling against a scream. For heaven's sake, he was *obsessed* with sex. For once, couldn't he just be my agent and stay out of my love life?

# Twenty-Two

Some last autumn leaves still clung to the branches, embers of red and gold. It was to be my first visit to Michael's manor house. Michael thought it was time that I met Amelia. I was hoping fervently that she would accept me as a friend.

The house, of pale stone, sitting in a valley in deepest Devon, had been built in 1760. In the spring it would be covered in clusters of blue wisteria, now it was cloaked in burnished Virginia creeper. It was hidden from the road by a dense forest. The grounds, large parts of which had been left wild, were beautiful, and a small river gurgled through them.

Amelia was like a sketch drawn with a fine crayon. Sixteen years old, tall, willow slim, with a lively face and large, dark, intelligent eyes. She had a poetic quality, the kind of face one sometimes sees in paintings of medieval maidens. Long reddish curls tumbled to her waist. A little birthmark, the colour of a ruby, glistened on her top lip. Her finger nails were chewed to the nubs.

The death of her mother had blackened her life, but even before that grief she had led a fractured existence. Somewhere between babyhood and puberty she had mislaid her joy. She had been sent to three of the top schools in the country, but couldn't settle in any of them. Her mother had been the only person who could make her feel safe. It had been rebellion on all fronts. But you would never know it from how she looked that moment: sweet sixteen, with the grace of a figure in a dream.

Michael introduced us, a look of curiosity on her face. She leaned towards me with an outstretched hand. 'How wonderful to meet you!' she said, her eyelids fluttering.

I took her hand, beaming. But inside my thoughts were jumbled. Would the image of her mother stain our lives? Her little face, white as cream... I felt a sudden responsibility. Here was a young girl with a chunk of her soul missing. Whatever I felt, whatever I wished, I had to be careful with her – careful, and truthful too.

Michael had informed me that Amelia was a budding artist. I asked her if she was working on anything at the moment, and without further ado she linked arms with me, and led me inside the manor, towards the grand staircase.

'You're an actress, Papa says,' she breezed. 'Will you teach me how to make my face up like Anouk Aimée? How wonderful that you're going to make my papa happy again.' She continued, sweetly hopeful, in this manner, all flighty fragments and sudden bursts of enthusiasm, all the way to her bedroom, where one by one she showed me her paintings. How marvellous, I thought to myself, things are going so well.

A couple of days later we left Michael with his 'brain work', and Ameila led me along the banks of the river. The slowly flowing water looked like dark grey silk.

'I've never seen my Papa cry,' Amelia said suddenly, seemingly out of nowhere. 'Even when Mama died. I never saw him with his arms around Mama, the way he does around you. He used to make my mama cry.' She broke into a nervous giggle. 'He drinks too much. Mama hated the smell on his breath. So do I.' Then in a sudden burst: 'Parents take everything for granted!'

What did she mean by that? By any of it? It had all come out in one big jumble, her tone slipping from honeyed to heartbroken. I waited for her to continue, but she was silent.

The few days I had spent in Amelia's company had been enough to make clear that this was her pattern. At any moment she might erupt, bursting forth with emotional outpourings, isolated images from her memory. I thought that she must have been yearning for someone to share these feelings with for a long time. 'I loved Mama, I had to learn to love Papa. When I was little, he would never let me ride piggy back...' I was to be her sounding board, it seemed. Though I was unsure how I should help her, I was touched by her trust.

The girl had the nervous energy of a sparrow. She flitted down to the water's edge, then darted away, calling out, 'Biscuit! Biscuit! I want you to meet my stepmama!'

Suddenly a towering chestnut horse emerged into the clearing along the riverbank.

Amelia bounded back to me. 'Biscuit is my very, very best friend,' she said, her eyes bright with earnestness. 'He knows all my secrets.'

'Do you have many?' I teased. 'What are they?'

'Silly! If I told you then they wouldn't be my secrets anymore!' She wrapped an arm around Biscuit's neck and whispered in his ear, 'Love-you-love-you-love-you-love-you!'

She had love to give, and in giving it to Biscuit, she felt safe. Oh, the guileless heart of the lost, the confused... She drew him closer.

Her other horse, she informed me, was called Freckles. 'Bob has him, the stable boy. He's away being re-shod. He's golden brown and a bit old now. He'll be back tomorrow. We could go riding. Up early, out on the moors before breakfast. Such fun!'

Keeping a watchful eye on Biscuit, I informed her that I had been nervous of horses since filming a scene set in a farm yard. I had been handed the reins of this horse, with the assurance that she was docile. Quietly sitting astride her, while the crew busied themselves setting up the shot, I had been thinking of my dialogue when the animal had decided to head back, at a trot, to her stable. The floor of the stable was littered with old machinery, and the top half of the door to her stall was closed. To fall to the floor, or to collide face-first with the wooden door? I decided on the former and threw myself to the ground, which I hit with a wail, the stone bruising my lower back. I suffered dumbly through the filming, and as bad as the pain was, excruciating in fact, I didn't tell anyone, thinking of that actor's mantra: be a pro.

Throughout my story, Amelia's expression never wavered. She stared at me with a sort of ecstatic determination. 'You simply have to get back up,' she said, once I had finished. 'It's something we can do together! It's perfect! I'll help you get over your fear of horses, you help me with Ophelia.'

She had been cast as Ophelia in her school's production of Hamlet. 'I love her,' she'd told me. 'I think I understand her, but the words are so hard. There's so many! I always run out of breath!' I had told her that I'd show her how to breathe from her diaphragm. 'Perfect-perfect-perfect,' she'd kept repeating, clapping her hands.

This advice I was happy to give. As for the horse-riding... But Amelia was offering me something, a gift, the gift of her youthful enthusiasms. I vowed, at all costs, that it would never be me to dampen them.

At dawn, out in the yard with Amelia, Freckle studied me, his ears pricked. Amelia had reassured me that he was 'Safer than a cradle', but I was not convinced. His eyes looked spooked to me.

'Does he come with a guarantee?' I asked, my nerves making my forced laughter sound brittle.

Amelia helped hoist me into the saddle and weighed me up with a raised eyebrow. She led us slowly around the yard, instructing 'Toes in, reigns over, under. Nose down, backside up. Keep moving! Knees tight, dig them in Backside down!' The whole hokey-cokey of equestrian jargon. It was clear to anyone with one blind eye that I was anything but a natural, but she was indefatigably cheery. 'See?' she called. 'It's great! You're doing great!'

Ignoring my protests she bounded up onto Biscuit's back and shepherded me towards the open gate. I went bumpity bump, bumpity bump down the lane, trying to control the restless Freckle with sweet talk. 'No, no, Freckle, you don't want to jump that fence. No, not into the river. Easy boy, whoah there!'

'Trot on,' called Amelia. 'Give him his head!'

'Are you kidding!' I yelped. 'My bum is throbbing! It feels like a squashed potato!'

'You mean two squashed potatoes!' she fired back.

Back in the yard, feeling almost tipsy with laughter, I half slid, half fell to the ground.

Amelia, giggling, stooped to help me stand.

With perfect timing, Freckle, as if to tell me 'Good riddance!' let out the loudest, smelliest fart. Michael must have been able to hear our hysterics from his study, because when we returned to the house he was in a mood.

That evening, sprawled on a velvet, dog-hair covered sofa, I thought of putting on some music, something cosy. But no, the sound of the log fire was all the room needed. At dinner, Amelia had been given her first taste of gin. She had taken a bird-like sip, then shaken her head fiercely. Spitting it back into her glass, she had declared it vile.

Now as we sat in contented silence, suddenly she chirped up again.

'Are you going to have a baby one day?' she asked.

'Well...' I said. 'We'll have to wait and see.'

It was a tactful reply, considering Michael's... particularities. But Michael, now on his third whiskey, seemed not to hear. 'Not a chance!' he said, wiping his chin with his blue-and-white-spotted handkerchief. 'I can't get it up for love nor money!'

I was mortified, clutching my glass in horrified silence. Oh, God, let him shut up! But, thank heavens, Amelia seemed oblivious of his meaning.

'Oh, Papa,' she said, 'you're so silly.' But then all at once her face hardened. 'But what does that mean?'

'It means, dear daughter, I know what I know... what I know!' This was a statement that seemed to call for another drink.

Amelia's features took on a pained expression. She persisted, 'Oh, Papa, you're never serious with me. Why can't I ever have grown-up talks with you?'

A long second stretched. With frustration she continued. 'I know you're proud of my artwork, but you don't know me. And I don't know you.'

Now it was Michael who seemed oblivious. He patted her knee absently, grunting.

'When I was little,' she continued, 'why didn't you ever let me ride piggy back?'

Another snort, a reflective pull of the lip and nothing more. Sober, Michael could be charming. But in his cups, he was often a bully and an insensitive bore. Anything emotional he called 'hearts and flowers nonsense'. A drinking man is not one person but two, and it's a battle of wits between them.

Straining every nerve to sound upbeat, I leaned towards Amelia and interposed, 'We'll be a happy family of three.'

Together we watched the fire for a while, in uncomfortable silence.

'What time is it?' Michael said eventually. 'Carruthers needs his last piss.'

Closing his glasses case, he stood, and his three grey-whiskered black Labradors, Montgomery, Carruthers and Winston, stretched and followed him, tails slowly wagging, to the door. 'Come on, boys,' he said to them. 'Let's leave the girls. They want us out of their way most of the time anyway.' But before he disappeared, he turned, smirking. 'And no more damn talk of squawking sprogs!' he remonstrated, and then bellowing '*Monty!*' he slammed the door behind him.

Amelia sat there, rocking slightly back and fore. Then she turned to me. 'Those dogs are the love of Papa's life.' she said, and at her sudden lucidity, and the look in her eyes, a chill ran up my back. 'Mama told me that when I was born, he said "I want a boy, push her back up".' She struck a fist into her stomach and burst into tears. I rushed from my seat and held her in my arms as she curled into a tight little ball. 'I miss my mama,' she sobbed.

Deep currents roiled within her. She was waiting for someone to fathom them. 'I miss her so much!' I had no answers. I felt so small, so helpless. But

I knew, sitting there, that I'd found my purpose in life. Her name was Amelia. She was giving me her love, her need. *Take my love*, I thought. I told her, promised her, that she would never, *ever* be alone again. That all the pain, the tears would end. That I was here for her and always would be.

# Twenty-Three

There were several rooms to be shuffled around. Michael and Salina's rooms had been interconnected, both on the same floor and overlooking the south rose garden. Each had a bedroom, a small sitting room and a bathroom. Michael suggested that I convert Salina's room to a kind of walk-in wardrobe.

But for Amelia to see another woman in her mother's private space… Had enough time passed? It might be more than she could bear.

So one day, as we were walking through the labyrinth of corridors, some of them crooked as a dog's hind leg, some of them so unused that you could flick a light switch and blow a fuse, I put it to her gently. 'Darling, Papa says I have free reign to decorate Mama's rooms.'

She studied me for a second, then without a word, took me by the arm and led me to her parent's wing.

'I haven't been in here since Mama died,' she whispered, stepping into her mother's bedroom. She looked around as if searching for something. Then she bounded over to a large chest of draws and took from it a cushion stitched with the words 'Tread softly because you tread on my dreams'. She hugged it to herself.

'Would you like to have Mama's rooms,' I asked her.

Beaming, she clapped her hands together. 'Could I?'

'Of course! You'll be able to help me choose the colours and pick the—'

'But you,' she interrupted, her expression suddenly serious, 'where will you sleep?'

'Well,' I said, hesitating, 'there are so many bedrooms. We're a bit spoilt for choice.'

She chewed her lip for a second, looking concerned. Then she held out the cushion. 'I made this for Mama at school. It's yours now, it's absolutely yours.'

We held each other close. 'Never forget to dream, darling,' I whispered. 'And *never* let *anyone* tread on your dreams.'

I felt my insides writhing with words unspoken, and knew that inside Amelia was in the same turmoil.

But then in my brightest voice I said, 'We've got so much to decide! I'll give Imogen from Colefax and Fowler a ring, ask her to bring over some fabric swatches and colour charts.'

I suppose it was only to be expected that her father would have his objections.

'You've done what exactly?' he growled, that evening after the three of us had retired to the sitting room. His voice was icy, falling on every word with a cold, dead weight. The room suddenly seemed so much smaller, oppressive. 'This is intolerable. You're telling me that you have given *your* rooms to *her?*' He waved an arm at his daughter, as if she was nothing more than a troublesome stain. 'You're ganging up on me. Am I nothing in my own house? Don't I have a say in this? I am absolutely not having it. *Fuck*, what exactly is my position in this love-fest? What are you trying to tell me here? Christ Almighty, am I never going to be number one?'

Head bowed, eyes brimming with tears, Amelia rushed from the room, the door slamming behind her. The sound of that door filled the house.

Unperturbed, Michael continued. 'Is that your plan? I'd have to make an appointment to see you?' His voice broke as he spoke.

I'd hurt him, I realised. I accepted the full heat of his disappointment. 'I'm sorry, Michael. I didn't mean to reject you. But she's a child... Where a child is concerned my heart rules my head.'

I stood and walked over to him. He avoided my eyes. I touched him lightly on the sleeve, murmuring, 'I wasn't thinking straight.' I admitted I'd lost focus, had forgotten about him, his needs, his feelings. I had heard his stories, after all. His mother had adored his brother. Amelia had adored her mother. Would anyone ever adore him? He was crying out, *Won't you love me? Love me, love me...* He had acted like an overbearing bully, but still I felt sorry for him. He needed me. Needed my approval, needed my love.

But I'd known love, true love, and there was a world of difference. I could have screamed it at him then, screamed it at him so he would never forget: 'I love Steve! Not you! Steve!' But then I remembered Amelia and swallowed the words like bitter pills.

*

I snuffed out the storm that had been brewing by sleeping in his bed that night. I stole away from the sitting room early, before he was accustomed to going up to bed. Standing in front of his long mirror, I pulled off my pants and bra and, shivering, examined myself. When did I this thin? Of course, I had never been heavy, but I didn't want to lose my breasts. They'd always been, as casting agents never failed to remind me, my 'best bits'.

Tucked up in Michael's bed I heard his footsteps on the stairs. He opened the door and stood in the doorway, frozen at the sight of me.

'Josephine,' he said.

Wordlessly, I pulled back the covers. An invitation.

Some nights he would want to sleep in my arms as a baby would. He would tremble all night. Or he liked to sleep curled up behind me, a hand on each of my breasts. He liked to squeeze them, to suck on my nipples. Or he'd have me sit naked in front of him, and he'd reach out and timidly slap them. The Polaroid camera I'd given him for a birthday present was kept in his bedside cupboard, along with a notebook and pen. After any sexual contact he'd write a tick. 'I want to get to a hundred by Christmas,' he'd say. Oh, shut up.

Occasionally he'd ask me to hide somewhere. I'd go to a different room, crouch in the cupboard or climb under the bed. The longer he had to search the more excited he'd become. On finding me, he'd wrap his hands under my arms, half lifting me up from my knees, or drag me by ankles into the light, and in his whiskey-thick voice, he'd growl, 'Beautiful tits, beautiful. Mine...' Then he'd suck on them with a need that sometimes frightened me, lick, suck and flick them as I remained entirely passive, my thoughts running mechanically round and round. Alcohol and my hidden stash of marijuana saved my sanity more than once.

Before me, he had said, he had been inclined to prostitutes, thirty-quid-a-time girls with rent to pay, kids to feed. No questions asked, no numbers or names exchanged. He once admitted he never knew how Amelia had ever been conceived. He even suspected that she wasn't his. Perhaps that was why he kept her at such a distance. I felt my care for her double at this revelation. Amelia, darling innocent Amelia. I had no love for Michael, but I loved her already.

No, this wasn't a rampant affair. But I had been lucky – I had known love. Now it fell to me to give it – to spread love through this ancient, windbitten home. Here was going to be my life: our home, our future. I would stand by this man, and perhaps in time there would be music, we would laugh and sing.

It might sound fanciful, I know, but I wanted to bring light into this house, with all its ghosts and stories. I felt I had this to give this lost little girl and her dad. No, you couldn't call him her dad. Her *father*. A songful of difference.

I felt tender towards Michael. But I never loved him, not for a moment – not love as I'd known it. I could never even utter the word, even to spare his feelings. And I never had even the tiniest interest in him sexually. When I was with Michael there were always echoes of the other men I had known. Simon…

*'I was the first man to make you come.'*
*'How do you know I wasn't faking it?'*
*'Were you?'*
*'Says a lot about you that you couldn't tell.'*

And Steve… Never out of my heart for a second. Ours a love undying. Then Mace, lost alcoholic, but beneath all the machismo, a sweet soul…

Their faces, their bodies would run through my mind as I passively allowed Michael to do whatever he needed to. Sometimes they made me sad, wistful. But my life was no longer solely mine. There was Amelia, desperate, tortured Amelia, calling out to be saved. My rock and roll days were gone. My life of shits and giggles were to be but a memory. As Willie Nelson said, 'Turn out the lights, the party's over.'

So, of course, when Michael asked for my hand, I said yes.

# Twenty-Four

I had only five days in London to prepare for our wedding. Of course, my first port of call was to see my mother. Her decline had been precipitous. She just couldn't live without my daddy. I'd been paying for her to be cared for in a home, but I needed to reassure myself that she really *was* being cared for.

I bought some lovely flowers and a large box of Malteasers and was shown into the conservatory. My mother was sitting in a chair, a pink blanket tucked around her knees, squinting against the early spring sunshine.

I approached her cautiously. 'Mummy, it's me. Mummy...'

To my dismay she looked at me with an expression of sheer horror then let out a cry. '*Nurse!*'

A male nurse appeared, blonde, with arms as big as hams. He took her hand gently. 'Who is this woman?' my mother demanded, 'Calling me *Mummy?*'

The nurse answered her gently, 'It's Josephine, your daughter. She's come to see you.'

My mother dropped her chin to her chest and scrutinised me out of the corner of her eye. I moved towards her slowly, timidly, wanting to soothe her, but she shrank away.

'Who *are* you?' she hissed. 'Calling me Mummy. I'm not a grown up. I'm not a *mummy*. I don't have a *baby*. I don't *want* a baby.'

She struggled to get up, the blanket falling from her shoulders. Reflexively, I threw my arms around her to keep her from falling. For a brief moment I held her like a lost child. She had become so thin – she was almost nothing but the material of her dress and cardigan – barely more than a handful of feathers

'Get your hands off me!' she screamed. 'You're hurting me!'

'Oh, Mummy, please,' I cried out to her, 'don't do this to me!'

She pushed me away, her strength, in her desperation, surprising me. Her eyes glazed over, she called out, 'Andrew! *Andrew!*'

She was asking for Daddy. A moment later, her eyes were closed and she was shaking her head wearily. 'Why, Andrew?' she asked. 'Why?' Again and again and again.

For a long time I stood by the door to the conservatory, watching my mother staring into space. She was peaceful now, oblivious of my presence. I was listening, praying a little. Sobbing. I don't know which. The nurse went about his rounds. He paused alongside her for a moment.

'My princess likes to sing "Anniversary Waltz",' he said to her softly.

Looking off into the dimming twilight of her days, her hands moving as though she was conducting a band, she rasped back: 'Oh, how we danced...'

'So the limp-pricked sod's hoping to make a lady out of you?' said Kenneth with his usual steeliness. He liked nothing better than to see me squirm. Sometimes a meeting with him felt as if I was standing at the business end of a cannon.

But not today. No way.

'That's the idea!' I responded breezily.

'Christ, his last wife, poor bitch, drowned herself, you know.' Sweat gleamed faintly on his forehead. 'He's the worst thing ever to happen to you.'

'No chance of a wedding present then?' I shot back.

'He still can't get it up, I suppose?'

Throw a punch, receive a punch.

'You seem remarkably informed. Are you both members of the same clubs? Not exactly the Garrick, White's, the Reform. More... Churchill's, Shepherd's Market, Soho Swingers. The less salubrious ones. Do you sleep with the same prostitutes, I wonder? What a laugh.'

I'd found the sharpest words. He raised his eyebrows. I could tell I had gone too far. But ah well, he'd had this one coming for a while.

'How lovely for you,' I continued. 'Do you double date? Discuss the stock market over a couple of whiskeys? Well, you'll need those for the courage to face the girls. Mammoth tits, full bush over their sopping cunts. Breath on your face, hands on your body...' I looked him up and down. 'Ooh, do you like to be tied up? You do, don't you? I'm right, I know it. She ties you up, sits on your face. You feel dizzy, long for air. Struggle to get free, but it's all for show. And then your sad old prick can't take it anymore, so it's out with the thirty quid. Or perhaps you're given a discount on account of your age?'

Now it was my turn to torture. I could have kept on, but I had to pause for breath. Kenneth was already heaving himself out of his chair. 'Get out of my office,' he spat, his jowls trembling. 'Out of my sight.'

Out in the street I puffed on a cigarette, feeling my career sliding further into my past with every drag. And you know what? I couldn't have cared less. 'Fuck him,' I said aloud. 'Fuck it all. Past, present, future!'

Michael had given me his credit card. Did I go on a spree? You betcha sweet life. But that evening – my second to last back in London – as I collapsed onto my bed, shoes kicked off, bra unhooked – I had one regret. I had been peppering the phone of my Victor for days, but it seemed like he had dropped off the face of the earth. But when I reached out and clicked the answerphone, there was my darling old queen himself.

'Josephine,' he declared, 'it's time to celebrate you jumping off the spinsters' shelf! Tomorrow at Sheekey's, twelve thirty. Last one to arrive has to have two puddings!'

Irrepressible as ever, it seemed Victor wanted one last blowout.

J Sheekey was a seafood restaurant set in a side street between two of the most successful West End Theatres, a little like the more famous Sardie's in New York, Broadway's 'to be seen' hot spot. Many glasses have been raised to hits in Sheekey's, and many a sorrow drowned at reviews.

Victor was there when I arrived, looking pink and chipper, his fat arse perched precariously on a stool at the bar.

John, the renowned maître d', greeted us as dear old friends. He directed us to Victor's usual table, situated under the black and white photographs of Britain's post war screen legends Kenneth More and Jack Hawkins.

I ordered halibut, no starter. Victor did not even have to speak his order. John just asked, 'The usual?' and he nodded with a wink. His 'usual' began with a large portion of whelks – and that was barely the appetiser.

After a large glass of Pinot Noir he looked me straight in the eyes, and to my surprise, I saw that he was on the verge of tears. 'Are you in love with him?' he asked.

After a long moment, I answered. 'No,' I said, 'I'm not. But I do care about him. I think we'll rub along OK.'

He rooted in a bowl for an olive. 'You've one life, Josephine. Are you sure you're not throwing in the towel?'

'Victor,' I said, 'It's for the best, really. No, it's not perfect but... what else is there?'

The wine had started to speak for us both now. 'Oh, Josephine, when did you give up believing in fairy tales?' Victor said, his voice breaking a little. 'You have standards, talent, dreams. I know your type, and it's not weak-chinned wankers. You're my darling friend. I don't want to lose you...' Then suddenly he snapped upright, alert, as if coming out of a daze. 'Oh, enough already,' he said. 'I'm wasting my breath anyway. Look, here's the main course.'

My friends' dislike of Michael wasn't difficult for me to understand. I wasn't insensitive to their reasoning. After all, I'd told them straight up: I wasn't in love with him. Sometimes he did a number two in the loo and forgot to flush! And I knew what had happened to his first wife. But I am a determined Scorpio female. History might tell that the only person ever stung by my tail was myself, but I had never pretended to know where I was headed. All I was doing was all I had ever done: throwing my hands up in the air and beseeching my friends to throw caution to the wind, to take the world by surprise, to dance side by side with me and watch me go.

# Twenty-Five

It was my last day, and my diary looked like a railroad map. Minute by minute the tasks accumulated. First over to Bruce Oldfield's showroom, to collect the slip of a dress he had designed for Amelia: a wisp of silk the colour of a Mediterranean sky, calf-length, almost Grecian. Good old Bruce. It was simply dreamy. When I had shown Amelia the sketch, her face had glowed with sheer delight.

'It's too amazing… *Amazing*. Can I go barefoot?'

'Yes, darling,' I'd said, 'but we should see to those toenails first! Perhaps I should get Bob Oates to have a go at them?'

'Bob Oates?' she'd exclaimed, 'but he's our blacksmith!'

I smiled. 'Exactly my point!'

Her father was letting her wear some of her mother's jewellery: delicate teardrop diamond earrings and a single string of pearls. 'Only for the day,' he kept repeating, emphasising each word. 'Only for the day.'

Amelia would roll her eyes to the sky. 'Alright, Papa, I heard you the first time.'

Then to Edina Ronay's showroom for my dress. Oh, I wish I could draw it for you. I'm not exaggerating when I tell you it was stunning. As Ed presented this white vision to me, it seemed the dress almost drifted up into the air. I had asked for a '50s look: knee-length white silk tightly nipped at the waist, forming an A-line from the front, but from the back becoming full-skirted with petticoats. A corset sewn in so it could be worn off the shoulder, it was unadorned apart from a two-inch crystal belt.

I couldn't help but squeal, seeing it for the first time. 'It's a real film star's dress!' I jumped up and down, kissing Ed and her husband, Dick, until their cheeks were sticky with my lipstick. I expect I was babbling, making as much sense as an agnostic priest mumbling through mass.

Next it was Turnbull and Asser, in Jermyn Street, for a new shirt for Michael. Kenny Williams, the manager, greeted me with pleasure. 'Josephine, darling, we've heard you've fallen for a prince.'

'You heard wrong, Kenny. Not quite a prince – an earl!'

The look on his face was priceless. As I was leaving with my packages he gave me a hug, a joke curtsey, and a free tie for Michael as a wedding present.

All was going my way. Just one last stop at Armour and Winston in the Burlington Arcade just off Bond Street. I'd spied something I thought I'd buy for Michael as a wedding gift. Sitting in the window on a blue velvet tray was a gold Regency stickpin, a tiny duck with a dark green enamel head, dinky gold feet, and its body a cluster of diamonds. It seemed the perfect thing. Then it was time to quit spending. I'd almost come to the end of my budget.

Liz, Liz, I had to see my unfailing friend. The sky now grey, at four in the afternoon I arrived in Fortnums, where she was waiting for me. I placed a blue Tiffany box in front of her. Her hands fumbled with the white satin ribbon as I urged her to 'Open it, open it!'.

'Oh, Josephine,' she said, lifting the lid and peeking inside, 'what have you gone and done now?'

Her eyes shone as she withdrew the two twinkling diamond ear studs. 'Oh, Josephine, wow. But are you sure? They're really too good for me.'

I reached across the table, taking her hand in mine. 'Nothing is too good for you. I wanted to spoil you. You've been the best of friends to me.'

We were both sniffing into our tissues already. But what else are best friends for? We went on in a sentimental vein. 'Friendship is the wine of life,' I'd say.

'Oh, what a good idea!' she'd fire back, giggling. 'Let's have another.' And she'd wave vaguely in the direction of our waitress.

'Oh, Josephine, you've always been like a bird,' she said at one point in the evening, 'flying high.'

'High,' I whispered, 'but not away.' I looked her straight in the eye. 'Let's face it, Liz, we know far too much about each other – we'll have to be friends for ever!' We both laughed in a little burst of pure joy.

'Are my secrets safe with you?' she asked.

'To the grave,' I said, 'like mine with you.'

'Oh, I don't know,' she said with a wink. 'Yours might be worth a bob or two to the *News of the World*!'

There is security in friendships that have stood the test of time. Once when I was in the West Indies, I saw a little blue and yellow fishing boat. On the side had been painted the words 'Old friends is best'.

'We'll have blow out dinners,' I promised Liz then. 'We'll have fireworks, we'll have parties by the pool.' I clasped her hand in mine. 'I won't disappear.'

The thread of our shared histories ran between us, vibrating with emotions like a direct line from her heart to mine.

The street lights were already on, lights still twinkling from the sop windows as we headed for home. The number fourteen bus breezed past us, and Liz had to break into a run to catch up with it. 'I love you, Josephine,' she called out over her shoulder.

'Me too you,' I gasped out after her, but she was already swinging herself onto the bus. It ground to a halt at the lights, and I chased after it, craning my neck, searching for her face behind the windows, but she must have gone up to the upper deck. I was professing my love to no one.

# Twenty-Six

A s I pulled into the drive – the house as I approached it could still take my breath away – there he stood, dripping with rain, his head bare, his shoulders hunched. Seeing me, he hurried forwards, holding out his left hand with his heart in his eyes.

And in his right hand the largest white teddy bear I had ever seen! It must have been at least two foot. And Michael had hung around the teddy's neck a rope of aquamarines and pearls! Our eyes twinkled at the ridiculousness.

'Have you had a wonderful time?' he croaked. I realised that the strength of his emotions was choking him up.

'I have, I have,' I said breathlessly.

'Did you miss me?'

Clutching my teddy, I put my free arm through his. 'What do you think, silly? Of *course* I missed you.' I gave him my softest smile. But it wasn't true. I hadn't, not at all. He laughed, but looked perturbed. Did he feel that I was leaving something unsaid? Oh dear, I thought, I'll have to do better than that,

In the morning, I gave Michael, still in his silk pyjamas, his presents. With every item he unwrapped, he said the same thing: 'You've spoiled me.'

Of course, he'd also spoiled me something rotten, giving me the most perfect pale blue Smythson's jewellery box. It had its own tiny lock and key, little drawers and different compartments, and in each of the compartments one of his family's jewels: in one a platinum and sapphire bracelet, in another a double string of pearls, in another two diamond rings, and in the last, ruby earrings red as the colour of blood. On the lid of the box he'd had engraved in his own handwriting, 'Nothing is forever, except us – let's do something wonderful together'.

I gave Amelia a soot black French poodle puppy. I'd had to smuggle him up the stairs the previous day, keeping him quiet through the night with generous bribes of biscuits. Amelia immediately christened him Memphis. 'Can he sleep on my bed?' she pleaded, cradling him in her arms.

And between us, Michael and I had bought her an up to date music system for her room. 'Just what I wanted,' she squealed, Memphis briefly forgotten.

She set it all up and took it for a test listen. The volume turned up to max, Linda and Richard Thompson singing 'I Want to See the Bright Lights Tonight', she spun around the room, holding out her arms towards me. 'I do love you, Josephine,' she shouted over the hullabaloo.

I watched her for a moment before I followed her father down the stairs. She smiled at me, and I blew five kisses to her. She had said, I think, what she had been trying to say all these weeks, but for which she hadn't until now found the perfect time.

Michael had asked Father Xavier, our local Catholic priest, if he would conduct our wedding ceremony up in the big house. Father Xavier had been a Jesuit intellectual, but for whatever indiscretion, religious or otherwise, he had been farmed out to minister to our hamlet. He'd always been a shoulder for Michael. The story went that his sermon at Salina's requiem mass had made no mention of the cardinal sin of suicide. Of course, Xavier was in Michael's pocket. But it was a deep pocket, and I liked the ruminative father, who had been a huge help in introducing me to the community.

The ceremony was small and intimate, just Michael, me, Amelia, our dogs and our witnesses: the groundskeeper, Oates; the head gardener, de Winter; the stringent housekeeper, Mrs Schick; and the cook, Mrs Bell.

We were married at six in the evening, in the library. The room was lit solely by candlelight. Flowers in every vase, on every surface that could hold them. The log fire burned and crackled in the cavernous grate. Oh, I thought to myself as I stepped into the room, it's going to perfect, completely perfect.

My ship had been tossed on many stormy seas. Was this my harbour?

'Hold my hand, hold on tight,' Michael said, as we stood together in front of Father Xavier.

He had a way of looking at me sometimes that was so full of feeling that you could forget he wasn't very good looking. We stood there together in the candlelight, our hands loosely clasped, returning each other's looks, promising to hold each other dear, no longer separate, no longer alone.

Afterwards, we opened the champagne and cut the cake. Mrs Bell had made a chocolate sponge covered with meringue, decorating it with fresh flowers. Michael played a strident beat on the piano, looking up at me the whole time.

On my second glass of champagne, rather theatrically, I began to sing along, '*Do I love you? Oh my, do I? 'Deed I do…*'

I was a little bit tipsy, my voice not pitch perfect by any means. But who cared, we were having fun. Amelia was sitting watching me, smiling, her eyes bright, calling for an encore. Memphis bounded about the room, yipping with glee.

It was sunshine then. But in the back of my mind, that old refrain kept going round and round…

*Do I love you? Oh my, do I?*

# Twenty-Seven

The next few months were blissful laziness and contentment. Sometimes, when I was out riding Freckle, or walking the dogs through the woods, or waiting for Amelia to come home from school, I'd wallow in my memories, feeling wistful for my past life. For film sets and the stage. Challenging, exciting times. Those times seemed so long ago now. But I never allowed myself to dwell for too long. It was only ever a moment, quickly evaporating away.

Amelia was showing a fresh love of life, barrelling through the house, Memphis at her heels, giggling her special little giggle – a sound as delicate as the bells on Santa's sleigh. I spent much of my time helping her to prepare for her drama exams. The plan had been for her to go to New York to study art, if she could get the grades. But during the past few months, drama had taken her fancy, and now she was planning on auditioning for RADA. I might have been biased, of course, but I believed she had real natural talent. I encouraged her, but I tried not to be too pushy: the whole world was before her, and it was early days to set one's plans in stone.

She was my darling daughter, my reason for being, my baby bird with a broken wing. I simply wanted her to be happy. And so she seemed. Until one afternoon I found her sobbing on her bed.

'Darling, what is it?' I asked.

'Misty says I'm a thief!' came her plaintive voice from under a pillow.

Misty was her best friend. They had known each other since they were babies.

'Just what are you meant to have taken?' I asked.

'Her silver Tiffany pen,' she wailed through her tears.

'Oh, that's just silly,' I soothed. 'You have one of your own!'

'I know!' she said angrily, sitting suddenly upright. 'I was using it in class.

She saw it. But she's convinced it's hers!'

Gradually I coaxed the full story out of her. Misty had marched up to her after class. 'You crazy bitch,' she had screamed, 'that's my fucking pen!' Amelia had protested, voices had been raised, accusations flung. A heavy hush had fallen over the other students as a sobbing Amelia had ran from the building.

'Don't break your heart over it, little one,' I told her. 'I'll call Misty's mother. Catherine, isn't it?'

She nodded, her eyes teary.

I wiped away her tears and tried to lift her spirits. 'Anyway, crying will give you a shiny red nose and pink eyes – not a good look!'

Her sobs quietened a little, and she even offered me the faintest of smiles.

'We'll get to the bottom of this,' I reassured her, smoothing her hair. 'I'll ask them both over for tea.'

Amelia caught her breath. 'Oh no, Josephine, I don't want to see her ever again!'

'It's no use arguing,' I said firmly. 'You've done nothing wrong. We're going to head this quarrel off at the pass.'

I told her how my father had taught me to always 'kill 'em with kindness' – it was the best way of disarming someone.

Crossing the room, I made a final remark over my shoulder. 'You'll learn: sometimes the best of friends make the very worst of enemies.'

# Twenty-Eight

Don't trouble yourself to wonder what tomorrow might bring – you never know when your life will collapse around you like rubble. For me it was one night in late June, while Michael and I were cuddling, him the big spoon, me the little one, on the verge of sleep.

'Are you cold?' Michael asked.

I wiggled closer, and his arms tightened around me.

He made soft kissing sounds into the nape of my neck, cupping his hands over my breasts. Suddenly his kissing sounds died away. I thought he had drifted off to sleep. But then he spoke:

'Josephine, you have a lump.'

I reached over for the light, clicked it on, and we both sprang out of bed. I rushed over to the mirror, letting my nightdress fall about my heels.

There was no shocked moment when I first felt the lump. A bolt didn't swoop down from the sky. I just felt my heart dissolve in my side.

My knees felt ready to sink. I let out a soft cry: 'Cancer?' Fear trickled in then. I turned to Michael, hoping for reassurance, telling myself, *relax, we don't know anything for sure yet.*

*You fucking bitch!*' he spat. 'You expect me to believe you've never felt that before?' A cruel smile bent his mouth. 'You treacherous little cunt! You married me knowing you had cancer!'

He punched the wall , his limp prick swinging with the sudden movement. A picture fell – and with a final look of disgust and contempt, he stormed from the room.

I stood there stunned, like a snowdrop in a storm. He was crazed, mad, a mad thing. His suspicion of me knew no bounds.

That word, 'cancer', seemed to hang in the air, swelling to fill the space Michael had vacated.

Over the next three days, I finally found out what Michael was really like, what he really thought of me. His cards were in open view, out on the table. In those days I experienced the full force of his anger.

He was stone deaf to my protestations. He believed I'd trapped him. He was indignant, outraged – he wanted me gone, and he spelled out in no uncertain terms that this 'farce of a marriage' was over.

I spent much of my days pacing the estate, alone, thinking of Steve.

When the hour appointed for my departure arrived, Amelia came meekly into my bedroom. Her body trembling, looking at me intensely, she grasped the back of a chair for support. When she spoke, there was a note of terror in her voice. 'Josephine, what about me?'

I made her a promise that she could come and stay with me in London whenever she wanted. 'I'm not leaving you, darling,' I said, my voice choking up. 'It's just that Papa doesn't want me here.'

I heard my taxi blare its horn. I clutched onto my suitcase. We held each other for a couple of moments. Then she ran from my room, her face in her hands. The door swung on its hinges behind her. The sound of her sobs echoed in my mind for days.

As the taxi turned out of the drive, and the house was lost behind trees, I knew I was leaving things on a knife edge. Amelia, who for so short a time had flickered into life, would be left alone in darkness again. The house would become quiet, cold as a grave, the corridors stalked by the mourning ghosts of this ancient family.

# Twenty-Nine

Horror. Nightmare. Amelia was dead. *No, no, no...* It can't be, *couldn't* be. Like her mother before her, she'd taken some stones from the yard, crammed them into her pockets and walked into the lake. Her body was found lodged up against the sluice gates, her long hair rippling in the water. Michael didn't even call. Such coldness... It stabbed like an icicle right into my soul. Only Father Xavier thought to let me know, sending me an edition of *the Times*, Amelia's name in the obituaries section. Already she was yesterday's news.

I had joined my life with hers. She had believed that I might fill the missing part of her, the wound her mother had left. And then I, too, had abandoned her.

Was it the hand of her mother, reaching out across the darkness to draw her daughter into her arms? Or was it my arms pushing her into the darkness? Darkness take us both. Her laughter rang in my ears, her crying...

Tests. More tests. Scans. More scans. Blood taken. More blood taken. I started to call the hospital the Vampire Clinic.

I was sitting across from my four eminent specialists. Their charm practically oozed. I suppose that was partly what you paid for – to be put at ease. But I was in no mood for their pleasantries. I had just been told that the tumour Michael had found in my breast was a secondary, that the primary cancer had spread from my bones to my lymph nodes and then to my breast. How could they answer, how could they soften the truth when I so baldly asked, 'So, gentlemen, am I riddled with it?'

They could only look appropriately, self-consciously grave as they nodded their heads.

I felt myself mentally withdraw from the room. Outside of the window was a garden. Summer clouds scooted across the sun, casting shadows. The fresh new leaves still trembled with a recent shower. Everything was just coming to life. And here was I.

'Shit, gentlemen... Pardon my language,' I suddenly blurted. I studied their faces, so professionally concerned. My every nerve tingled. I felt fear, and something I couldn't put into words. Then it came to me like a whisper in the dark: what I needed to say. I pulled my shoulders back, straightened my beret, adjusted my clothes.

'Morphine in the handbag for me, please.'

Dead quiet.

The doctors stiffened, but didn't say a word as I told them that I would refuse all radiation, all chemotherapy – all treatment of any kind other than to ease my discomfort. They puckered up their eyes as though they were staring into spotlights. Then one of them reached forward and patted my hand. 'You'll come round,' he said, as if delivering a verdict.

That's what you think.

It was time for me to go. Love is nature's painkiller, and *my* love? Daddy gone. Amelia gone. Steve gone. Mummy lost in another world.

This might appear to be Josephine the actress, starring in a one woman exhibition of 'Look at me, look at me! Aren't I brave?' It isn't. I'm not.

Let the waves carry me where they will...

With the morphine, sometimes I feel transparent. I am standing in front of my window with only a nightie on. I don't feel the slightest bit cold. Someone is with me. I close my eyes, and I'm dancing around the kitchen, my feet on Daddy's shoes. *Teach me, Daddy, show me how.*

And Steve. He is always with me. Watching over me. Waiting for me.

Victor and Liz are helping me, making it possible for me to stay in my own home, not a hospice. Taking it in turns, with me around the clock. Sometimes they'll ask, 'Josephine, shouldn't you have a trained nurse, I mean really, shouldn't you?'

'No,' I answer, 'all I need is you.'

I've made out my will, and to them my apartment, my car, my books, my precious things, my everything. Most of all, my gratitude.

If I think of Michael, and I don't often, all I see is one swollen varicose vein. I've returned all the jewellery he ever gave me. His response was to ask if I had taken three of the manor house's monogrammed bath towels. Oh, shut up.

Brittle. I broke my thumb peeling an orange. I don't walk, I limp. Fatigue of body, fatigue of spirit. Morphine, more and more of it, and none of it enough. Crawling off like a small, wounded animal. That's not how I want to go. The actress who didn't quite make it, the daughter who went her own way and lost herself, the woman who loved a man and lost him too...

Time takes us all. Why wait? I have a plan. It has to be today. Liz has gone to see her mother, Victor his accountant. Alone till at least three. At all costs I mustn't involve them. This isn't a conspiracy. This is my decision.

I have been saving my pills. I count them out. Eight, nine, ten. Will it be enough? Let's see...

I swallow them in one gulp. Scrabbling around in my drawer, I find a tube of stale Smarties. Sweetness drives out the foul taste of medicine, of poison. I slip on my pink-silk eye shades. I'm settling down. I want sleep, deep and soundless sleep.

In the neighbouring garden, I can hear music. Someone's playing a harmonica, each note so perfect, so pure. Children's voices sing 'Happy Birthday'. I can hear my own voice, but it's so far away, as if it has travelled ahead. To be with Daddy. To be with Steve. To be with Amelia and to wait for all my other loves to join us in time. Nothing really ends, does it?

With me on my bed. I've photographs of my parents, of my little dog, of Amelia with Freckle. My old teddy bear is next to me. Under my pillow a dog-eared copy of *Alice in Wonderland*.

The birthday singing fading to a buzz, the sunlight to black.

My head feels too heavy to lift. My legs start shaking uncontrollably. I've done my research. That'll be the nerves breaking down. I'm not frightened.

Now a warm laziness relaxes me. For every down, an up. Swings and roundabouts. No regrets.

I've pressed it all to the limit, trusting always that my life would turn for the better. That one day soon I'd be riding the breeze, flooded with offers, rave reviews, my life a ray of light, a silver shooting star, sparkling with camera flashes. Ah, almost... almost.

Fade to nothing. Now my thoughts are gossamer-light, like ice-blue butterflies on the wing...

# Acknowledgements

My warmest appreciation goes to my editor, Will Rees, for his patience;

Kenny Laurenson, for designing the stunning artwork;

Nick Pourgourides, my publicist, a complete professional
and a good friend;

Felicity Green, Douglas Rae and the late John Goodwin, for their
encouragement and enthusiasm.